The Exact Location of Home

★ "Vivid characters and situations, along with clear, simple writing and plotting, make this an accessible and enlightening read."
—*School Library Journal*, starred review

★ "Middle school worries and social issues skillfully woven into a moving, hopeful, STEM-related tale."
—*Kirkus Reviews*, starred review

"Sensitive and realistic." —*Publishers Weekly*

The Brilliant Fall of Gianna Z.

E. B. WHITE READ ALOUD AWARD WINNER
AN INDIE NEXT LIST PICK
A BANK STREET BEST CHILDREN'S BOOK OF THE YEAR

"Laced with humor and heart." —*Booklist*

"An engaging saga." —*Kirkus Reviews*

"Messner's warm and humorous tone will capture even reluctant readers." —*School Library Journal*

The SEVENTH WISH

A *KIRKUS REVIEWS* BEST MIDDLE GRADE BOOK OF THE YEAR
AN NPR BEST BOOK OF THE YEAR
A NERDY BOOK CLUB BEST MIDDLE GRADE BOOK OF THE YEAR

★ "Hopeful, empathetic, and unusually enlightening." —*Kirkus Reviews*, starred review

"An empathetic, beautiful, magical, fiercely necessary book."
—Anne Ursu, author of *Breadcrumbs* and *The Real Boy*

ALL THE ANSWERS

"Charming, moving, funny, and ultimately very surprising!"
—Wendy Mass, *New York Times* bestselling author of *11 Birthdays*

"An emotionally resonant portrait of a sweet girl whose
struggles are firmly rooted in reality." —*Booklist*

Wake Up Missing

AN INDIE NEXT LIST PICK
AN IRA INTERMEDIATE FICTION HONOR BOOK

"Combines a fascinating concept with page-turning suspense."
—Margaret Peterson Haddix, author of the Missing series and
the Shadow Children series

"Mystery, intrigue, danger, and creepy futuristic science set in
today's world? Yes, please!" —Lisa McMann, *New York Times*
bestselling author of *Wake* and *The Unwanteds*

EYE OF THE STORM

AN INDIE NEXT LIST PICK
A BANK STREET BEST CHILDREN'S BOOK OF THE YEAR

"A suspenseful science fiction story that keeps the reader engrossed
from beginning to end." —*Library Media Connection*

"Plenty of action. . . . These heart-pounding scenes
will be a hit." —*School Library Journal*

Sugar and Ice

AN INDIE NEXT LIST PICK

"A title that remains in your mind long after
you've put it down." —Fuse 8

"Satisfying and likely to have wide appeal." —*Booklist*

The Exact Location of Home

Books by Kate Messner

The Brilliant Fall of Gianna Z.
Sugar and Ice
Eye of the Storm
Wake Up Missing
All the Answers
The Seventh Wish
The Exact Location of Home
Breakout

The Exact Location of Home

KATE MESSNER

BLOOMSBURY
CHILDREN'S BOOKS

NEW YORK LONDON OXFORD NEW DELHI SYDNEY

BLOOMSBURY CHILDREN'S BOOKS
Bloomsbury Publishing Inc., part of Bloomsbury Publishing Plc
1385 Broadway, New York, NY 10018

BLOOMSBURY, BLOOMSBURY CHILDREN'S BOOKS, and the Diana logo are trademarks of
Bloomsbury Publishing Plc

First published as an e-book in December 2014
Hardcover first published in the United States of America in September 2017
by Bloomsbury Children's Books
Paperback edition published in September 2018

Bloomsbury books may be purchased for business or promotional use. For information on bulk
purchases please contact Macmillan Corporate and Premium Sales Department at
specialmarkets@macmillan.com

ISBN 978-1-68119-898-9 (paperback)

The Library of Congress has cataloged the hardcover edition as follows:
Names: Messner, Kate, author.
Title: The exact location of home / by Kate Messner.
Description: New York : Bloomsbury, 2017.
Summary: Believing his long-absent father is missing and leaving clues behind
through geocaching, Zig, thirteen, relies on his love of electronics, a garage
sale GPS unit, and his best friend, Gianna, to search for answers.
Identifiers: LCCN 2017008520 (print) • LCCN 2017030022 (e-book)
ISBN 978-1-68119-548-3 (hardcover) • ISBN 978-1-68119-713-5 (e-book)
Subjects: | CYAC: Geocaching (Game)—Fiction. | Fathers and sons—Fiction. |
Mothers and sons—Fiction. | Single-parent families—Fiction. |
Homelessness—Fiction. | Electronics—Fiction.
Classification: LCC PZ7.M5615 Ex 2017 (print) | LCC PZ7.M5615 (e-book) |
DDC [Fic]—dc23
LC record available at https://lccn.loc.gov/2017008520

Book design by John Candell
Typeset by Westchester Publishing Services
Printed and bound in the U.S.A. by Berryville Graphics Inc., Berryville, Virginia
2 4 6 8 10 9 7 5 3 1

All papers used by Bloomsbury Publishing Plc are natural, recyclable products
made from wood grown in well-managed forests. The manufacturing processes
conform to the environmental regulations of the country of origin.

To find out more about our authors and books visit www.bloomsbury.com
and sign up for our newsletters.

Every year, more than two million kids in America are homeless for a period of time, trying to make friends, get along with their families, go to school, do homework, and stay strong—all without a stable place to live. This book is for them.

CHAPTER 1
Short Circuit

He's not coming.

The thought's been buzzing around my brain all day like a mosquito that gets in the tent on a camping trip. It comes back, no matter how many times I swat it away.

I write my name on my English paper. *Kirby Zigonski,* and today, I add the Jr. at the end.

Kirby Senior will be here in less than twenty-four hours.

Dad's coming this weekend.

I start work on my essay and try to ignore the mosquito, still whining. *He's not coming.*

Finally, I make it to science, where I can forget about everything except electrons. Eighth-grade science is the best. Today, we're talking about circuits.

"A simple circuit is a beautiful thing," Mrs. Loring says,

tapping a link on her whiteboard to show us a website. Some of the kids laugh at that, but I lean forward. Mrs. Loring is absolutely right.

The great thing about a simple electrical circuit is how everything fits. If something is wrong, you can see it right away, and you can fix it. There's only one path the electrons can take, and no matter how many little lightbulbs or alarms or motors or buzzers you connect with your wires, the electrons still have to travel that one path. If there's a problem, the whole thing shuts down. But as soon as you find it and fix it, everything works.

All or nothing. I love that. Electricity makes sense.

That's why I stop to pick up the toaster at Mrs. Ward's garage sale on the walk home from school with Gianna and Ruby. There's a bunch of broken kitchen stuff in the free pile.

"Doesn't your mom already have a toaster?" Gianna pokes through the pile and pulls out a little wood frame with no glass.

"Don't you already have a broken picture frame?"

"You don't want glass in the frame for acrylics." Gianna puts the frame in her backpack. She picks out a purple plastic flower, too, and tucks it into her hair. The wind blows and buries the flower in a pile of red frizz. She might never find it again.

"Yeah, we have a toaster," I say. "But look—it's almost new. She probably tossed it because of a short circuit. It'll take me ten minutes to fix."

"It'll take me less than that to destroy you in a rock-skipping contest." Ruby pulls us off the sidewalk into Rand Park, where there's a little beach. She loves skipping stones. She wishes on them and says if the stone skips ten times the wish will come true.

"Make a wish, Zig." Ruby hands me a stone the size of a hockey puck but thinner.

I drop it at her feet, unskipped. "Too windy. Even if you calculate the angle perfectly, there are too many variables with the waves. It won't work."

Gianna whips her stone out over the water without even aiming. It skips twelve times.

"Well done!" Our neighbor Mr. Webster smiles at Gianna under his white mustache as he walks by. I used to see him out walking every morning when I was doing my paper route, before Mom's schedule changed and I had to give it up.

"Thanks, Mr. Webster!" Gianna waves. "I *am* the skipping master, you know."

"More like the lucky-throw master." I tug her backpack so we can get going. "Come on, I'm starving. Mom said they'd have pie at the diner."

A great blue heron flies along the shore, like it's daring us to a race. I speed up a little but then trip over the toaster cord.

"Want to go garage-saling tomorrow?" Gianna bends down, scoops up a handful of horse chestnuts, and tucks the shiniest ones in her coat pocket. "Pretty soon it's going to get cold, and people will stop having them. I need to find some ribbon and stuff for Nonna's memory book."

"How's she doing?" Ruby asks.

"Okay. She hasn't wandered off again since we had the alarms put on the doors. And she likes the adult day-care center where she's going on weekday mornings now. They have a ton of people there with memory problems. I think she has a boyfriend."

Ruby nudges Gianna so she almost stumbles into me. They laugh like "boyfriend" is the funniest word ever.

"What's so funny?" I ask.

"Nothing," Gianna says. "Want to go to garage sales tomorrow or not?"

"Can't," I say. "Dad's coming."

I try not to smile all goofy when I say that, but I can't help it. I haven't seen Dad in more than a year because he's been traveling so much. He buys and sells property, so he's always taking trips. Last year, our Christmas weekend got called off because of a strip-mall project in Florida, my birthday party ended up being the same day as a closing on an apartment complex in Boston, and our June camping trip got replaced by a weekend in Maine to check out property on a former air force base.

The thing about Dad is that it's hard to be mad because he's so awesome when he finally shows up. When I turned eleven, he came in a limo with pizza and a cooler of sodas in back and took all the guys at my birthday party for a behind-the-scenes tour of the IBM factory. Granted, "all the guys at my birthday party" consisted of me plus Hassan and Evan from science club, but I was a rock star to those guys for a while. When Dad shows up, the circuit is complete. The lights go on.

"You're not camping this time, are you?" Ruby zips her jacket as we turn the corner and the wind picks up. It's still September, but when school starts in Vermont, snowflakes are never far behind.

"Nope. We planned this weekend at the beginning of summer when his last visit got canceled. Dad's flying in tonight, and I'm spending the weekend with him at his hotel. He's gonna have a huge suite, and we're building this awesome computer from scratch. Don't say anything to Mom. She gets uptight when Dad buys expensive stuff."

I open the diner's glass door, and a warm cloud of sweetness swallows us up. Alan's Diner always smells like pancakes and maple syrup. Ruby, Gianna, and I have been coming here to do homework after school every day since Mom took a part-time job as a waitress to help pay her nursing school bills.

We take our usual booth in the corner. Ruby plops down on one of the red vinyl benches. I slide onto the other one and set the toaster next to me.

Gianna glares at the toaster like it's in her spot. She's been sitting next to me lately instead of with Ruby. She came over to get help with math one day, and now it's sort of permanent. That's not bad or anything. Just different. I lift the toaster up onto the table next to the saltshaker and ketchup so Gee can slide into the booth.

Mom's busy waiting on a big table. She looks up and gives a little wave, tucking a lock of hair behind her ear. She looks tired, like she was up late studying again.

Mabel brings our hot chocolate. "There you go, kiddos." She squirts the whipped cream on top of each mug, turns to make sure Alan's busy at the grill, and then squirts some right into Gianna's mouth.

"That is so unsanitary," I say. Gianna's laugh sends bits of whipped cream spraying across the table. We reach for napkins at the same time, and our hands bump. I pull mine away.

Mabel grins. "Easy there, Zig. She won't bite you. You kids have any big plans for the weekend?"

"My dad's coming up. We planned everything over the summer. We're going to build—" I catch myself. She'd tell Mom about the computer for sure. "A model airplane, I think."

"Well, you have fun." Mabel hustles away to clear another table, just as Mom arrives with three slices of apple pie.

"How was school?" Mom asks. Usually, she scoots in and sits with us a while if it's not too busy, but today she's kind of hovering.

"Good," I say, like always.

"We got our science tests back," Gianna says. "Zig got an A-plus."

"That's great," Mom says.

"Hey, Mom, what time is Dad picking me up in the morning?"

She takes a deep breath. "We need to talk about that."

The mosquito in my brain is back, buzzing away, but I keep talking.

"Is he in town now? Maybe he can pick me up tonight."

"No."

"So what time—"

"Zig, he's had . . . kind of a wild week."

My eyes drop to my plate. I've heard it so many times she doesn't have to say it. But she does.

"He's not coming."

CHAPTER 2
Disconnected

Friday night, I try calling Dad's cell phone. I get a message that it's no longer in service. My e-mail to him bounces back, too.

"What's going on with Dad?" I ask Mom when she finally gets up Saturday morning. I've been at the table trying to fix this stupid toaster since I woke up at seven, but I can't figure it out. It shouldn't be this hard.

Mom walks past me to the kitchen counter. I know I should give her time to make a cup of coffee since she worked at the diner all day and then had class until ten last night. But I have to know. "Why isn't he coming? And how come his phone's not working? Does he have a new number?"

Mom pours creamer into her coffee, sips it, and adds more coffee. "I don't know. Last time we spoke, he called me from a different phone because he was . . . traveling. And there's a—he had a land deal that—one of his projects created a bit of a problem."

"Which one?"

"A new one. You haven't heard of it." The screen door opens and closes, and Mom sets her coffee down to grab the newspaper. She doesn't read it—just tucks it under her arm.

"Can he come next weekend?"

"I'm afraid not."

"Is he going on another trip? Maybe I could go with him, because—"

"No." Mom clangs her spoon down onto the counter and turns so fast some of her coffee sloshes onto the floor. "Just no." Her look says *quit asking*. The doorbell rings, but Mom doesn't move to answer it. Instead, she reaches for a paper towel to clean up the coffee. She yanks so hard the whole roll flies off onto the floor.

I hand it back to her and answer the door.

"Hey!" Gianna's dressed in her garage sale clothes—jeans and an old gray fisherman's vest with lots of pockets for change. She got it for a quarter at a church rummage sale last spring.

Ruby's carrying a newspaper, folded open to the garage sales listing page, and a little blue pillow with red flowers on it. "Mom wants me to find another cushion this size for a dining room chair."

"Let me get my jacket and some money." I have to step

around Mom. She's scrubbing the floor hard for such a little coffee splash.

"I'll see you later, okay?" I tell her.

"That's fine. Have fun."

I let the door slam on purpose and glance back. That kitchen floor tile is spotless. And Mom's eyes are red as she watches us leave.

CHAPTER 3
Jam Jars, Jewelry, and a GPS

"Can I help you find anything?"

"No, thanks, just looking." The ad in the paper said this sale had "miscellaneous electronics," so we came here first, but I've pawed my way through three tables of jam jars, tablecloths, and old necklaces, and I have yet to see a single gadget.

"Are you looking for a gift for someone? Because I have some lovely teddy bear figurines over here . . ." Garage Sale Lady points to a shelf with dozens of little ceramic bears. She walks over to them and pats one on the head as if she's the mama bear.

"Aren't these adorable? They're a terrific deal . . ." She flashes me a smile like the ladies at the jewelry counters where Dad used to shop for Mom.

"Uh . . . no, thanks."

Ruby and Gianna laugh and fish through a laundry basket full of scarves.

An ambulance siren wails, getting louder and louder until it zooms past the driveway and down the street. Gianna looks up from the scarves for a second and frowns. Nonna is home today, not at the center where she goes when Mr. and Mrs. Zales are working.

Nonna's memory has gotten a lot worse lately. It started with dumb stuff: cookies left in the oven too long, false teeth in the fridge. But then last fall, she got really lost one afternoon. I know Gee worries about her.

"Do you like to read?" Garage Sale Lady shoves a worn copy of *Charlotte's Web* into my hands. I look down at the cover. Wilbur's laughing at me.

So is Gianna, who's trying on an orange-jeweled frog pin from the jewelry table. I take a deep breath. "Do you have any, um, electronics? The ad in the paper said—"

"Oh!" Garage Sale Lady looks sad all of a sudden. "George loved electronics . . ." She blinks really fast and then sighs. "I decided it was probably time to get rid of some of his things, though. He passed away in April."

I look at my shoes. What am I supposed to say? I didn't even know George.

Garage Sale Lady squints at me. I get the feeling that even if she is selling George's stuff, I'm going to have to pass some kind of test to prove myself worthy. What do I do? Hug her?

Ruby saves me. "I'm so sorry about your husband," she says,

putting a hand on the woman's shoulder. "My grandma died a year ago, and I miss her, too. Mom says it helps to share good memories."

Garage Sale Lady sniffs and smiles a little. "My George was a wonderful man. He could fix anything."

"So can Zig." Gianna steps up to us, wearing the frog pin on her green hoodie and a purple beret on her head. "He made an alarm for his backpack so Kevin Richards can't get in to steal his math homework anymore."

Gee grabs my backpack and almost pulls me over trying to unzip it.

WHOOT . . . WHOOT . . . WHOOT . . . The alarm goes off.

Ruby laughs and wanders away to flip through a box of albums.

Garage Sale Lady raises her eyebrows. "You remind me of George." She takes a deep breath and pulls a cardboard box from under the nearest table.

"I'm not even sure what he had in here," she says, opening the dusty flaps. "He used to tinker around in the basement for hours."

She steps aside, and I bend down to look into the most amazing collection of gadgets and parts and pieces in the universe. It's geek heaven.

There are wheels and motors, rolls of wire, toggle switches and button switches, batteries of every voltage level. Propellers. Motherboards from at least half a dozen computers.

I look up at her. "This is awesome."

She smiles into the box, then right at me. "Georgie would have liked you, Ziggy."

"Zig," Gianna corrects her, but I wave my hand. This lady can call me whatever she wants. I pull out a clock radio.

"Georgie fixed that." Garage Sale Lady reaches in and pulls out a string of Christmas tree lights. "And these. Whenever I had trouble with the lights, he'd fiddle with them till they were good as new."

"Did he use aluminum foil?" That's how I fixed our lights last year.

"Yes!" Garage Sale Lady claps her hands.

I dig deeper into Georgie's toy box. There's an AM/FM radio. An old phone. A few flashlights. Some whole. Some in pieces.

Gianna looks over my shoulder. The leopard print scarf she's draped around her neck dangles down and tickles my arm.

"Hey!" She reaches into the box and pulls out what looks like a little yellow radio. "It's one of those things Mrs. Loring showed us in science last week."

"A GPS unit?" I reach out to take it from her. "Does it work?"

"It will need batteries, I'd imagine," Garage Sale Lady says. "Georgie loved that thing. He said it was for some game."

"I bet he was geocaching!" I say.

Gianna snaps her fingers. "Mrs. Loring talked about that. People hide stuff—Tupperware boxes with little toys and things, right?"

"Yep," I say. "There are caches hidden all over the world. People enter the latitude and longitude coordinates on this website, and then other people use either their smartphones or a GPS unit to try and find the stuff." I hold up the GPS. "This tells you how far away you are and then points you in the right direction."

"Do you play this game?" Garage Sale Lady asks.

"Well, no. My dad's into it, though. He said he'd take me sometime, but we haven't gone yet."

"Huh," Garage Sale Lady says. "So what's this thing called? A Jeeps?"

"GPS. It stands for Global Positioning System," I tell her. "It sends out signals to satellites that are orbiting the earth and uses the position of those satellites to tell your exact longitude and latitude."

"Which is which again?" Gianna, who had wandered off into the racks of clothes, is back, draped in a fur wrap that still has a fox's head attached to one end. She reaches over and makes the fox sniff my ear. "I always forget."

I swat the fox nose away and reach for a dusty globe on the table. I run my finger around its circumference.

"You know lines of latitude and longitude are these imaginary lines that go all the way around the earth?" I ask. Gianna nods and reaches over to spin the globe. "Think about the word 'long' in longitude. Someone who's tall is very long, so lines of longitude are the long lines that go up and down around the globe. Lateral means sideways. So lines of latitude go sideways around the globe."

I turn back to Garage Sale Lady. "And a GPS unit tells you your exact location by giving you longitude and latitude."

"We used these to play a game in science," Gianna says. "Mrs. Loring gave us the latitude and longitude of a location near school, and we had to enter it into our GPS units. Once you enter a location, your GPS tells you how far you are from that location and then gives you an arrow, like a compass, showing which way you need to go to get there. We used ours to find a monument downtown."

"Well, how about that." Garage Sale Lady shakes her head. "Just amazing. You go ahead and take that box, Ziggy. No charge. I'd like someone to appreciate it like Georgie did, and frankly, I can't imagine anyone else wanting it."

"Thanks!" I say, and pack up the box. Some people don't know a treasure when they see one.

CHAPTER 4
Sirens and Lights

"Here, let me help you with those." Gianna pulls out a pile of '70s albums from the box Ruby's carrying.

"Thanks," Ruby says. She wraps her hands underneath the box, where the flaps are starting to sag open. "I can't believe she gave me all these." She peers into the box. "Journey. The Rolling Stones. ELO."

"I bet Zig would like that one . . . *Electric* Light Orchestra." Gianna laughs at her own joke. Then she stops cold as we turn the corner. The ambulance that screamed by is on our block. Gianna gives the albums back to Ruby and takes off. I set my box down in a neighbor's yard and run after her.

Gee's father is standing by the ambulance parked between her house and the house two doors down, where Mom and I rent our apartment.

"Is it Nonna?" Gianna's out of breath and almost crashes into her dad, she's running so fast.

He puts out a hand to catch her shoulder. "Nonna's fine, Gee. She's inside with Mom."

"Mom!" I run for the steps to our apartment. I knew it. She looked wrong this morning. I sprint up the steps, but before I get to the top, the door swings open. Mom holds it for the EMT guys. The first one backs out, wheeling one end of a stretcher onto the porch.

"It's Mrs. Delfino," I say when Gianna and Ruby catch up to me. "She lives upstairs."

One of the attendants holds an oxygen mask over Mrs. Delfino's face as the other one opens the back door of the ambulance. Ruby frowns as they lift the stretcher. "She doesn't look good."

She doesn't. She's pale. And quiet. Normally, Mrs. D can talk up a storm.

The siren wails again, and the ambulance heads down the block.

Mom takes a deep breath and comes down the porch steps to join us. Her dark hair sticks to her temples, and her face is shiny with sweat.

"What happened?" I ask.

Mom reaches out and brushes my hair out of my eyes. "Mrs. Delfino knocked on the door this morning. I suppose it was about the rent, but she never even said anything. Just stepped inside and collapsed. I checked her and couldn't find a pulse, so

I called for help and started CPR." She pauses and blinks away tears. "I never got her pulse back."

"It doesn't always work," Ruby says. She was there when her mom tried to do CPR on her grandmother last fall.

Mom looks at her and gives a sad smile. "I know."

We throw a frozen pizza in the oven and have a quiet dinner before Mom goes off to study. I head to my room and dump out George's box of stuff. Time to take inventory.

Two small motors. A roll of wire. A bunch of switches and a couple propellers—one big and one small. I wonder what George was going to do with those.

The big propeller is fantastic. I snap it onto one of the motors, find my wire cutter, snip off about four inches of wire, and strip the ends so I can make a connection.

I dig an old LEGO car out of my closet and duct-tape the motor with the propeller onto the back. I wire it up to a toggle switch and fish a nine-volt battery from the bottom of Georgie's box. I tape the whole thing together so no wires hang loose and take it down to the tile floor in the kitchen.

I kneel next to the table, set the car on the floor, and flip the switch. The motor whirs like a dentist's drill, the propeller spins into a blur, and the whole thing takes off across the floor toward the basement step, just as Mom opens the door and comes up with a big basket of laundry.

"Watch out!"

Mom tries to leap over the attacking LEGO vehicle, but the basket of clothes throws her off balance, and she crashes to the kitchen floor in a shower of socks and underwear. At least they're clean. Behind her, my propeller-car flies down the basement stairs, and I hear the heaviest pieces clunking their way down the steps.

"Sorry! You okay?" I ask.

"I'll survive." Mom laughs and starts collecting laundry. I help her pick up the socks.

"New invention?" Mom asks.

I nod. "It was a good one, too."

She laughs again. Her eyes don't look blotchy and sad anymore. It's better that way, so I decide not to bring up Dad again. At least not yet.

CHAPTER 5
No Good Answers

When I wake up Sunday morning, there's no pancake smell. Mom always makes pancakes on Sundays, but it's already 8:30, and the house still smells like last night's pizza.

I pull on sweatpants, grab my new GPS, and head downstairs.

Mom's sitting at the kitchen table with a bunch of envelopes and papers. She's poking at the calculator on her phone.

"What's up, Mom?"

"Oh! I'm just . . . straightening things up." She shuffles the papers into a pile. "You're probably hungry, huh? I'll make breakfast."

When she opens the fridge to get eggs, the cold light shows dark circles under her eyes. Mom stays up too late sometimes when she's studying for a test in one of her nursing classes, but I didn't know she had one this week.

"Mom?"

She whirls around, and the eggs slip from her hand onto the floor with a *crack-splat*. She says a word I've never heard Mom say before, and her eyes fill with tears.

"It's okay. I'll get it!" I grab the full roll of paper towels and start ripping them off, two and three at a time, to sop up the egg.

Mom reaches for the towels and helps me clean. "I'm sorry," she says. "It's been a tough week, and I didn't sleep last night. I'm a little jumpy, I guess."

She rescues two unbroken eggs from the soggy carton. "Pancakes?" She gets out the mixing bowl like nothing happened.

She must be sad about Mrs. Delfino, I decide. We found out last night that she died at the hospital, even though Mom had tried CPR. Like Ruby said, it doesn't always work. But Mom's about to become a nurse. That must have been tough for her.

Whipping pancake batter seems to make her feel better. She's humming as she ladles it onto the griddle, and now the house smells like Sunday morning.

The pancakes sizzle on the stove while I clear the table so we can eat. I set my GPS unit up on the counter and finish stacking Mom's papers into a big pile.

She looks up. "Oh!" She practically jumps over the counter to snatch the papers out of my hands. "I'll get those." She hugs them to her chest and hurries upstairs.

When she comes back, she picks up the GPS. "Where'd you get this?"

"Garage sale. A lady gave it to me because I reminded her of her husband."

Mom looks at the GPS like it's something moldy she pulled out of the fridge. She half laughs, half scoffs and turns to flip the pancakes. "Are you going off treasure-hunting like your father?"

"Mom, how come he's not coming?"

She slides the first four pancakes onto a plate and hands it to me. "We talked about this. He has things going on that make it impossible right now."

"What things? Can't I go with him?"

She ladles four more circles of batter into the pan. "No."

"But Mom, last time in Maine it was fine. You must have his new phone number or e-mail. Just—"

She whips around so fast she knocks the handle of the frying pan, and it spins around on the burner. "Enough, okay? It's not up to your dad. It's up to me. *I'm* the person who makes those decisions. *I'm* the person who lives with you and drives you to school and makes your breakfast, if you haven't noticed."

A haze of burned pancake smoke rises behind her. She takes a deep breath, smells it, and whirls around. She flips the whole frying pan over and dumps the pancakes into the trash. Then she turns and looks at me.

"I'm sorry. I'm sorry that you won't see him this weekend."

"I know. When can he come?"

"Maybe in a few months."

"A few *months*?!"

She puts her hand on my elbow, but I pull it back. "This time . . . it's different, Zig. It's . . . more complicated. It'll be a while."

"Why can't I have his new—"

"I'll help you arrange something when we can, okay? But let it go for now. Trust me on this one. Please?"

She brushes my hair back from my eyes and looks at me, waiting for an answer.

I nod.

But I don't promise.

CHAPTER 6

A Pile Full of Secrets

As soon as Mom leaves for her shift at the diner, I open the door to her room. The laundry is half-folded on the bed, and the papers and envelopes from downstairs are sticking out from under the towels. I sit down and shuffle through the pile. She must have Dad's new phone number here somewhere.

The papers are bills, mostly. $130 for Lakeside Gas & Electric. $80 for Northern Communications Telephone—and no number on the list of calls that looks like it might be Dad's. $467.42 for Mom's credit card bill. No wonder she's taking extra hours at the diner. I take a closer look at the credit card charges. Mostly groceries and gas. There's a big charge from the office supply store where we got my school supplies.

I flip through the rest of the pages. A few handwritten notes from Mrs. Delfino about rent. Mom must have paid it late this month. I'm about to replace the papers under the towels when a folded letter slides out from between two electric bills and drops to the floor. I recognize Dad's handwriting right away.

Dear Laurie,

I know you're aware of my current living situation, but I wanted to write you anyway, in the hopes that you won't judge. I never envisioned this, but life has a way of throwing curveballs. It will all work out.

I have plans to stay very involved in Kirby's life, as always.

Very involved? There's a thought.

I'd like to talk with him about this myself, so please don't cloud things with your spin on what's happened. It's hard enough. I'll be in touch soon.
—Senior

I stare at the signature. Senior.

That's Dad. He's Kirby Zigonski, too. When he was a kid, everyone called him Zig, like me. Now that there are two of us, they call him Senior.

I read his letter twice.

He has a new "living situation." How could he move and not tell me? Why would he be worried about Mom judging him?

The porch door slams and my stomach tilts. Mom must have forgotten something. I jump up, shuffle the papers together, shove them back under the towels, and pull the corner of the bedspread to fix the wrinkles I made sitting on it.

"Hey!" Gianna calls from the kitchen.

My heart settles back into my chest. "Don't you knock anymore?" I find her pulling a pitcher of lemonade out of the fridge.

"I did knock. But you didn't answer, and it was open." She pours herself a glass. "Want some?"

I shake my head. "Is Ruby hanging out with us today?"

"Maybe later." Gee downs half her lemonade in two gulps. "She has a Birds First meeting to talk about something with the herons at Smugglers Island."

"Oh." I watch her chug the rest of her drink. Then I remember the note upstairs.

"Hey, Gee, can I show you something in the bedroom?" She coughs on her lemonade, and I realize how bad that sounded. I feel my face getting hot. "No, I mean—something that's in there now. You don't have to go in there. In fact, you can't. You stay here. I'll go there. And I'll bring the thing back here. That I want to show you. Okay?"

I leave before she can answer. When I come back with the note card, Gianna's sitting at the table.

"You know how Mom told me that Dad couldn't come?" I say. She nods. "She won't say why and gets all mad and sad and stuff when I ask her. And she won't let me call him. His old number and e-mail don't work."

"Okay. So . . . ?"

I pull up a chair and hand her the note. "So check this out."

Her eyes skim back and forth. I reach for the broken toaster and start loosening the screws in the bottom while I wait.

"Sounds like he moved in with somebody," Gianna says, all matter-of-fact. She leans over to show me the letter. I push the toaster aside and lean in, even though I've read the letter four times already. Maybe she has a secret code to unlock it.

"See where he said *living situation*?" She points. "And then he's worried she'll be mad. I bet he moved in with his girlfriend."

"He doesn't have a girlfriend."

"When's the last time you saw him?"

"*Saw* him? A year and three months ago."

"A lot can change."

I take the letter from her and pick at the edges.

Dad has had girlfriends, but it's never been a secret. Why this time? How come he doesn't want me to know where he is? Unless it's somebody we know. Or maybe—

"Zig?" Gianna reaches over and puts her hand on mine. I look down. I've torn all the corners off the letter. She brushes the little paper bits off the table and throws them out. She picks up the GPS unit from the counter. "Have you tried this yet?"

I shake my head.

"Maybe we should go geocaching today! That game you talked about, where people hide things and you find them using . . . numbers and stuff."

"Satellite coordinates," I say. I can tell she's trying to get me to stop obsessing over Dad. She's probably right. "Remember that website Mrs. Loring gave us—was it geocaching.com?"

"Yep," Gianna says. "She said if you put in your zip code, it'll give you a list of geocaches near you. Let's check!" She disappears down the hall to the den where the computer is before I can tell her I need to get that letter back into Mom's stuff. I take the GPS and the letter and go back to Mom's room. I slide the note from Dad into the middle of the pile of papers and notice another handwritten note from Mrs. Delfino, dated four days ago.

Laurie,

I realize that this has been a difficult fall for you with nursing school, so I'm willing to let the rent go another month. Please be sure that the August and September payments are in the mailbox by October 1. Study hard, dear.

~Marietta

Wow. I can't believe Mom got so behind on the rent.

October first is three days away. Who's going to come pick up the rent check now that Mrs. Delfino is gone?

And what will they do if it's not here?

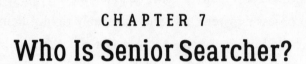

CHAPTER 7
Who Is Senior Searcher?

"Look at this!" When I get downstairs, Gianna has entered our zip code into the geocaching website. "Three whole pages of geocaches—all right in town." She scrolls up and down too fast for me to read anything.

"Hold still." I reach over her shoulder to grab the mouse, but she doesn't move her hand, so we're sort of holding it together, which is totally awkward, so I let go. "Just . . . don't scroll so fast."

From a safer distance, I read over her shoulder.

The geocaches all have weird names.

Nest Egg.

Where the West Was Won.

Cold Hard Cache.

The people who hid each cache have made up names for

themselves, too. Geocaching aliases, I guess. There are dates to show when each geocache was hidden and when somebody found it last. Some of them have clues, too, but the clues don't seem to make much sense.

"What's this picture of the Tupperware thing?" Gianna points to the screen.

"Dad told me people put little trinkets and a log book, and sometimes a disposable camera, in a waterproof container and then hide it in a hollow log or something. I bet that symbol shows you what it is you'll actually find when you locate the cache. Look." I point to one that looks like a globe. "It says this one's an Earthcache—a place you can go to learn something cool about geology."

"I want to find one of the Tupperware treasures." Gianna clicks on one called "Aromatherapy" that has the container symbol next to it. She squints at the numbers on the screen. "So if we plug these numbers into your GPS . . ." Gianna grabs a pencil and starts scribbling them down on one of Mom's sticky notes. "Then we can go there?"

I nod. "It's pretty close, I think." I enter our home base and destination coordinates into the GPS.

"Ready?" Gianna starts to close the website.

"Hold on. Let's print off the pages for a few of these caches, in case the first one doesn't work out."

"Okay." She clicks the back button and starts scrolling through the list again. I scan the titles, but nothing really catches my eye. I glance down the list of secret names of the people who planted the caches.

Mary Quite Contrary. Sirius Black. Bob Times Two. So Longitude.

I wonder what Dad's alias would be.

Gianna starts scrolling faster, and I catch a glimpse of something that makes my heart jump.

"Hold on!" I grab the mouse, scroll back, and click on the listing that caught my eye.

Gianna leans in to read the page. "Nest Egg? Think somebody stashed a log book in a bird's nest?"

"It's not that—look!" I point to the alias for the person who created the cache. *Senior Searcher.* It's a perfect code name for Dad!

"So?" Gianna tips back in her chair.

"Senior Searcher? Who do you know named Senior? My dad!"

"What?"

I tap the computer screen. "Gianna, he loves geocaching. He was always talking about taking me. I bet that's him! Remember, I'm Zig *junior.* He's Zig *senior.* Haven't you ever heard people call him Senior?"

Gianna puts the chair back on all four legs and looks at me. "I've only met him once, Zig, for about a minute and a half. At the fifth-grade picnic. Remember?"

I remember. Dad got there right as we were getting in line to leave the park and walk back to school.

"He was really nice, though," Gianna adds. "So you think this could be him? I don't know . . ."

"Look." I point to the screen name again. "It *has* to be him. It's too perfect not to be." I print the page. "Maybe if we find this cache, his new contact information will be in the log book, and I'll be able to call him or something."

"Maybe your dad will be stuffed in the Tupperware container, too."

"Gianna, I'm *serious*. This could help. It's all I have right now."

Gianna blows air up at her bangs. She stands and crosses her arms. "Zig, I'll go with you because I think the whole geocaching thing is cool. But I'm not convinced this is your dad. These names are all over the place." She leans to look at the screen again. "Sirius Black. Mary Contrary. Senior Searcher could be anybody."

"I know." I grab the pages off the printer. "But I want to get outside and get some air. Okay?"

"Sure." She smiles and pulls a rubber band thing from her pocket to put up her hair. It makes a big poof out of the back of her head. She pushes up her sleeves. "I'm off to find a treasure!"

"Me too," I say, and I reach for my backpack.

But what I'm really going to find is my dad.

CHAPTER 8
A Secret Cipher

"We should have tried Aromatherapy first. This one's impossible to get to," Gianna says.

We've been picking our way through the woods behind school for half an hour. Gianna ducks under a low branch and stops to pick burs out of her hair.

"Can I have those?" I hold out my hand for the burs.

She gives me a look.

"I like messing around with them. They're like supersonic LEGOs that never let go once you stick them together." I add Gianna's burs to the double helix I've made from the ones that keep sticking to my socks.

"What's that supposed to be?" she asks.

"DNA."

Gianna rolls her eyes. "Are we almost there?" She takes the

GPS from me and squints down at it. "Hey—it's talking in yards now instead of miles. Sixty-five yards this way." She points toward the riverbank where the trees start to thin out a little.

I take the GPS unit back from her and watch the number get smaller as we walk in the direction of the arrow. For a while, I forget about Dad and geek out over the science. I mean, this little yellow thing in my hand is sending out signals to *five* satellites orbiting the earth—sending out signals saying, "This is where Zig is in the universe." The satellites are sending signals back, and the computer uses all that to figure out my exact latitude and longitude. So cool.

"How far?" Gianna asks.

"Twenty yards."

"We're going to have wet feet in twenty yards." Gianna leads me to the edge of the woods, where a steep, crumbly dirt bank leads down to the river.

"Huh. The GPS unit still says five more yards, but that doesn't seem reasonable, given the situation," I say.

"That's kind of an understatement," Gianna says. September's been rainy, and the river is faster than usual for this time of year.

"Didn't Mrs. Loring say these GPS things aren't perfect?" Gianna says.

"She mentioned a margin of error, yeah." I look down at the GPS, wishing it would point back at the trees instead of into the river.

I take another step and feel water squish through my sneaker.
I hate margins of error.

"We must be close," Gianna says. "Let's look." She scrambles down the bank and starts looking into patches of weeds and picking up rocks. "Nope. Not there. Not there either. Nope. Nope. Nope." She puts her hands on her hips and looks up at me. "Are you going to help?"

"I'm actually thinking that it must be up here at the higher elevation. The area where you're standing would flood in the spring, and the cache is in a plastic container that would float away."

She climbs back up. "If I were a Tupperware container full of trinkets, where would I be?"

Where would my dad hide a geocache? I think.

"Hey!" Gianna says. "Was there a clue for this one?" She pulls the rumpled printout from the computer out of her jacket pocket. "Yes! It says . . . oh." Her nose wrinkles. "Brzoo kadeeya wer orn klik-jik dequig orz. *That* helps a lot . . ."

"It must be a code." Now I'm interested. "Let's see."

She hands me the paper.

BRX'OO KDYH WR ORRN KLJK DQG ORZ

"I've seen stuff like this before," I tell her. "It's a code where each letter stands for another one. You figure out how it works, and the new letters spell out the message."

"So you just start plugging in other letters? That'll take forever."

"Actually, the letters are only shifted. So an *A*, for example, might really be the letter that comes five letters later. We need to figure out what the shift is. Whether it's five letters off or three or what." I pull a pencil and yesterday's math homework out of my backpack.

"What are you, a secret agent? How do you know this stuff?"

"I read it in a book about spies during the American Revolution. They used codes so spies could carry secret messages that wouldn't be given away if they got caught. And they got the idea from ancient times. This kind of thing is actually called a Caesar cipher. Julius Caesar used it to communicate with his generals in ancient Rome."

I sit down in the leaves and lean against a tree trunk, studying the message. Gianna plunks down next to me and starts tossing leaves in the air. After a while, she leans over. "Got it yet?"

"Hold on. I'm looking for clues."

"Like what?"

"Like letters standing by themselves," I tell her. "A letter by itself has to be either an *I* or *A*, so you choose one. Let's say *A*. Then you can look at what letter the code maker is using to represent it, figure out how many letters away from *A* that is, and you've figured out the code."

Gianna looks at the scrap of paper in my hand. "There aren't any letters alone."

"No, but look." I point to the BRX'OO. "This has to be a contraction where the apostrophe comes before two letters that are the same."

Gianna twirls a maple leaf. "That would have to be *she'll*. Or *you'll*?"

"You got it," I say. "That means the code maker used *O* to represent the letter *L*. *O* comes three letters after *L*. So if we're right, it's a three-letter displacement. So every *A* is really a *D*. Every *B* is really an *E*. And so on." I scribble a quick chart under the coded message and hand it to her.

BRX'OO KDYH WR ORRN KLJK DQG ORZ

ABCDEFGHIJKLMNOPQRSTUVWXYZ
DEFGHIJKLMNOPQRSTUVWXYZABC

"Now can you figure it out?"

Gianna takes the pencil from me. She has it within a minute.

BRX'OO KDYH WR ORRN KLJK DQG ORZ
YOU'LL HAVE TO LOOK HIGH AND LOW

I read it aloud and look up. There's a hole in the trunk of the white pine I was leaning against. A perfect hiding spot.

"That's it! And he named the cache Nest Egg," I say. "It makes sense."

"It'd be a great spot . . ." Gianna doesn't sound so sure. "*If* somebody could get up there. But I can't imagine—"

"I know that's it!" I say. Dad would climb up there in a heartbeat. He's the one who taught me to climb the sugar maple in the yard at our old house when I was four. He climbed up behind me, and we sat way out on the branches and scared Mom when she came home from the grocery store. "That's him."

"Who?"

"I mean, that's it." I hand her the GPS unit and jump for a low branch. I miss the first time and my palms get all scratched up. The second time, though, I manage to catch the branch. I swing a little and fling one leg over it so I can pull myself up. I straddle the branch and shimmy over to the place where it meets the trunk.

The hole isn't that big. Probably not big enough for a plastic container, but to be sure, I wiggle a little closer. A bird comes blasting out of the hole, flapping and squawking right at my face. I duck to avoid getting my eyes pecked out, lose my balance, and fall backward over the branch. I clench my knees around it, and that's the only thing that saves me from landing headfirst on the ground.

I see Gianna from upside down. Laughing—no, *snorting*—the way she does when something's so funny she can't be bothered to laugh her more respectable laugh.

"Want some help?"

"No, thanks." Still upside down, I tuck in my shirt so my white stomach doesn't blind her. I reach back up to get a grip on the branch, let go with my legs, and drop down.

I land the wrong way on my ankle and fall forward onto my knees. Just as I start to stand, I see it.

A corner of blue plastic sticking out from the leaves blown up against the trunk.

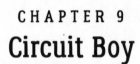

CHAPTER 9
Circuit Boy

"Got it!" I brush away damp oak leaves and pull out a Tupperware container the size of a shoebox. It's like the one Nonna keeps her recipes in.

My fingers are cold, so it's hard to get them under the edge of the lid, but finally I pry it off.

"Look!" Gianna says. She reaches in and pulls out a little green plastic army guy. "Stop!" she makes the army guy say in a deep voice. "I'm guarding this geocache. Do you have clearance to be here? Do you know the secret code word?"

I start to reach in, but Gee's army guy blocks me again. "I said halt. Don't make me use my itty-bitty plastic machine gun."

"Gianna, come on." I pull the box from her and paw through it. I push aside an *I Love Canada* key chain, a little plastic pig, a red whistle, one of those gumball machine bouncy balls, two state quarters, a tiny wooden airplane, a blue jay feather, and two polished rocks. There has to be a log book in here somewhere.

Gianna reaches over my shoulder, takes out the feather, and tickles me behind the ear with it.

"Quit it!"

"Have a little fun, Zig. It's a geocache. Not a top secret government file."

At the bottom of the container, under a tiny book of Robert Frost poems and a page ripped out of a cocker spaniel calendar, I find it. A little red spiral notebook with a golf pencil stuck in the rings.

"Are you logging our find?" Gianna puts the feather back and takes out the polished stones.

I don't answer her. I'm too busy scanning the entries in here.

Fantastic location! Enjoyed the hunt. We found it on the second try.
   ~Dumbledore and Dobby

Great cache! Took miniature Mr. Potato Head, left bouncy ball.
   ~Racer 14103

Had trouble finding this one... Came last winter in the snow and got too cold. Came back this spring. Got

wet feet but found the container after some searching.
Took arrowhead. Left Oklahoma state quarter.
   ~Daring Don

Came by to check on this one & happy to see that it's
being found by those who read the clues. Left a few more
goodies today—key chain & plastic pig. Happy treasure
hunting!
   ~Senior Searcher

"There he is," I think.

"Who?" Gianna says, looking over my shoulder. I guess I thought out loud.

"Look." I point to the Senior Searcher entry. "It's him. It's *got* to be my dad, Gee. Don't you see? It has to be. It's all so . . . him. The clue, searching high and low, the fake hiding spot in the tree. My dad would *love* knowing that he's sending all kinds of people up a tree for a phony hiding spot. He loves pranks!"

Gianna takes the log book from me. She doesn't say anything, but she frowns at it. "Does this look like his writing?" She hands it back.

I think about the writing in the note to Mom. It doesn't really look the same. That writing was all boxy and neat, and this is a little shaky. But then, that was a letter he most likely wrote with a pen at his desk, and this is a log book he signed in the woods with a tiny golf pencil. It was probably cold out. He might have had gloves on. If you consider all that, it sort of looks the same. "Yeah, it's his writing," I tell her. I look back into the box and pull out another clue.

"And look! This is what he left." I hold up the Canada key chain. "Dad and Mom took a trip to Quebec City after they first got married. That must be what this is from!"

"Zig, anybody could have left this." Gianna takes it and tosses it back in the box.

"We need to find another one," I say. I pull out the GPS and start checking the coordinates for Senior Searcher's other caches. "Maybe there's one nearby that we can hit before it gets dark. Somewhere, there's got to be something that'll help us figure out where he is."

Gianna reaches into her pocket and pulls out a refrigerator magnet of a little Picasso painting. She tosses it in the box, takes out the Canada key chain, and hands it to me. "Here," she says, and puts the lid back on the Tupperware. "You keep this one. But not because I think it means anything for sure. Just because I like maple leaves."

"Thanks." I put it in my pocket and help her brush the oak leaves back over the blue plastic box. We're almost back to the school when I think of something.

"Hey, can you hold on a second? I'll be right back."

"Sure." Gianna plops down on the grass and tips her head back to take in the last of the day's sunshine. I run back into the woods.

This time, the cache is easy to find. I pry the lid off the box and take out the log book.

> Climbed tree to look high. Fell out and looked low.
> Nice job, Dad. Call me, please.

I start to sign my name and then stop. Nobody uses a real name geocaching. I need a secret spy name. But one that's still me— one that Dad will *know* is me. I erase my *Z* and sign instead,

> ~Circuit Boy

Just in case he comes back.

CHAPTER 10
Birds First!

We get back to Gianna's house as her dad is arriving with the hearse to unload a body he picked up from the hospital morgue.

"Hey there!" Mr. Zales lifts one end of a gurney out of the back while their employee Phil gets the other end. Gianna and I follow as they push the stretcher into the back door of the funeral home the Zales run on the bottom floor of their house. Some kids at school tease Gee about her dad's business, but honestly, if you spend enough time around here, it feels like any other business. It's just that the customers are dead.

"Take Mrs. Rapazzo to the prep room, Phil, and tell her I'll see her in the morning." Mr. Zales gives a little wave to Phil and the body bag and then motions us to follow him into his office. "How's the hide-and-seek going? Gianna told me you might try geocaching today."

"It was fun," Gee says, picking a green apple from the bowl on the desk. "Zig fell out of a tree."

"Whoa!" her dad says.

"I'm fine." I say. "The GPS works great." I hand the device to Mr. Zales. "It took us right to the location."

Mr. Zales lowers his glasses on his nose and looks down at the screen.

"Guess what?" Gianna says. "We found a geocache guy who calls himself Senior Searcher, and Zig thinks—"

I kick her, and she coughs on her apple.

"I think the whole thing is really interesting." I give Gianna a *shut-up* look. Her parents are friends with my mom, and the last thing I need is her finding out that I'm looking for Dad.

"Well, good afternoon!" Gianna's Nonna twirls into the office in a bright purple dress. Gee says Nonna's Alzheimer's disease has been getting worse. She forgets a lot of things, but she still looks healthy. Today she's carrying a big plate of funeral cookies, which make her look even better. "Want one, young man?"

"Thanks, Nonna." I take a couple cookies from the plate. They're Italian wedding cookies to the rest of the world, but at the Zales house, they're funeral cookies. Nonna bakes them to share every time there are calling hours scheduled.

"Introduce me to your friend, Gianna." Nonna nods at me.

Gianna sighs, but she smiles. "Nonna, meet Kirby Zigonski. He likes to be called Zig."

"It's nice to meet you." I shake her hand for the third time in a week, even though she's known me since I was eight. It's better than telling her the truth and making her all sad because she can't remember.

"Thanks for the cookies, Mom," Mr. Zales says. Nonna sets down the cookies and lets him lead her back upstairs.

"Hey, guys!" Ruby appears at the door. She has an orange duffel bag over her shoulder with rolled-up poster paper sticking out of it. She looks down at the cookies. "Ooh! Nonna's been baking."

"How was your Birds First meeting?" Gianna asks. Ruby's the only kid in her birding and environmental action group, but she's fine with that.

"It was great. Really great." Ruby pops a cookie into her mouth and pulls a folded newspaper clipping from her pocket. "We have a new issue that's going to be huge. You're not going to believe this." She unfolds the article and hands it to Gianna. I read over her shoulder.

Development Threatens Rookery Bay Wildlife

Environmental activists gathered at City Hall last night to protest a condominium project planned for Smugglers Island. The project, approved by the zoning board and the State of Vermont two years ago, includes fifteen waterfront condominiums, a nine-hole golf course, and a club house on the former state land purchased by real estate magnate Henry Nicholson last summer.

"Things have changed on Smugglers Island, and this project needs to change, too," said Stephanie James, founder of Birds First, a regional bird-watching and wildlife protection group. "In the two years since the Environmental Board approved this project, a colony of great blue herons have established a significant nesting site at Rookery Bay, the location for the proposed project."

James said the herons moved to the Rookery Bay site after motorboat traffic disturbed their old nesting site farther south on the lake. She said the Nicholson project would involve clear-cutting twelve acres of Smugglers Island in order to make room for the condominiums and golf course. "These are the trees where the herons are nesting," James said. She showed the city council photographs of the heron nests. "If this project is allowed to continue, these birds will once again find their homes swept out from under them by careless people. I urge the council to take action."

Mayor Robert Bush said that the project had already received all necessary approvals and would move forward.

"That's it?" Gianna looks up from the paper. "Just 'Oh well, it already got approval, too bad for the herons?'" She has angry red spots on her freckled cheeks. I've seen those spots before. The mayor better watch out.

"I know." Ruby sets down her duffel bag. "My aunt Barbara is a member of Birds First, too. She says we're all going to protest at the next city council meeting and we can even go to Montpelier to do something at the state capitol if we need to. She says the guys involved in this development project are real dirtbags. I guess one of them's in jail because he hired somebody to cut down a tree on a golf course in Florida to get rid of a bald eagle nest that was in it so they could expand the course."

"What happened to the eagle?" Gianna asks.

"She flew away, but her eggs got destroyed when the tree came down." Ruby opens her backpack, and a pile of markers spills out onto the floor.

"Whoever did that belongs in jail." I bend down to get a marker that rolled under the desk. "What are these for?"

"I thought we could make posters that say 'The Herons Were Here First.'" Ruby hands Gianna a red marker. "Start lettering, okay?"

"I'll make one, but let's go upstairs. Dad has a meeting down here this afternoon."

"Zig, wanna help, too?" Ruby starts putting markers back in the bag.

"Nah, I'm going to head home. I've got research to finish for social studies."

Gianna pretends to be shocked. "You mean you didn't do your homework right after school on Friday?" Hers won't be done until first-period study hall tomorrow.

I wave and head home feeling a little guilty. But it was only a partial lie. I am going to do some research before Mom gets home. It just won't be social studies.

Unless geocaching counts as a geography lesson.

CHAPTER 11

Smoke and Deadlines

The answering machine light is blinking when I get home. It's Mom. Anybody else's parent would have texted, but I'm the only middle school kid in the Northeast without a cell phone, so she's left me a message here.

"Hey, Kirby. Mabel called in sick, and they offered me an extra shift, so I'm going to be late again tonight. I didn't get to the store, so there's not a whole lot for dinner, but you can fix . . . uh . . . I think there's stuff for grilled cheese and maybe a can of soup unless you ate it Friday. We have cereal, and I think there's milk, but check the date. Love you. I'll see you by ten."

I get a glass of ice water and plop down at the kitchen table. The toaster's still here from the other day, so I start sanding the electric connectors again. Maybe there's some crud on them that's messing up the connection. I sand them until they're perfectly clean and press down the button on the toaster to see if the coils heat up.

Nothing.

It figures, today.

I go to the fridge and pull out the American cheese. Even through the plastic bag, I can see mold growing on it. There goes the grilled cheese. There's not enough peanut butter for a sandwich. No canned soup. And Mom's right to be suspicious of the milk—it expired last Tuesday. Way in the back of the freezer is a personal-sized pizza. I unwrap that, toss it in the oven, and head for the office with a bag of stale pretzels.

At least I have unlimited screen time tonight. Mom's not here to come tell me my hour is up.

I go back to the geocaching website, to one of the cache pages Gianna bookmarked earlier, Aromatherapy. There has to be some kind of contact information for the people who hide the caches, doesn't there? What if one gets washed away in a flood or carried off by a bear? Wouldn't they need to contact the person who hid it?

Sure enough, all the user names are highlighted as links. Someone calling himself Dumbledore's Apprentice hid this one. I click on the name and end up on a profile page.

Jackpot.

Dumbledore's Apprentice, it turns out, is an earth science teacher from Horace Falls, ten miles away. There's a photograph of the guy with the Grand Canyon in the background.

Best of all, there's an e-mail link. If Dad's new address is on his profile, I'll be able to e-mail him. Maybe he'll even write back before Mom gets home.

I type Dad's geocache name, Senior Searcher, into the search box, click on the link for the cache we found today, and land back at the coordinates page that sent Gianna and me tromping through the woods, looking up, looking down, and falling onto the blue Tupperware box.

Dad's name is there—Senior Searcher—with a link to his page.

Before I click on it, I reach into my pocket and take out the *I Love Canada* key chain. It's smooth and kind of faded, like it got carried around in somebody's pocket for a long time. He and Mom were only married a year when they went on that trip. It would have been almost fifteen years ago. Before they had me. Before Dad got so busy traveling for business. Before they fought all the time about money and the risks Dad took with it. Before Mom decided she'd had enough.

I turn the key chain over in my hand. It's weird. I've heard Mom talk about this trip to Quebec. How much fun they had. How she laughed and laughed at Dad trying to speak French when all he took was a year of it in high school and he only knew how to order pastries and find out where the bathroom was. Mom said it was their best weekend ever. I can't imagine Dad dumping the key chain in a plastic box for some treasure-hunting kid to find, like it's junk.

But then I run my finger over some deep scratches on the

back of the key chain. I guess there was a lot of time after that trip that wasn't so good. They've been divorced three years now. Maybe he decided it was time to toss the souvenirs.

I set the key chain next to the computer, click on Dad's name, and wait for the profile to load.

Senior Searcher.

Where Dumbledore's Apprentice had uploaded a photograph of himself, Dad's profile shows a big, stupid-looking cartoon bug that says "No Image Selected" underneath. Where Dumbledore's Apprentice had a link to his e-mail address, Dad's contact information is listed as unavailable.

Occupation: Unavailable.

Location: Unavailable.

Dad's an expert at being unavailable.

I stare at the screen. There's a row of buttons at the top of the profile page that I haven't clicked on yet. *Profile. Geocaches. Trackables. Gallery.*

I click on *Gallery.* An error page says "No Photos Uploaded." *Trackables* sounds promising—I *wish* Dad were trackable—but that page is blank, too.

Geocaches is the only one left. My last shot at finding information. I take a deep breath and hold it. If I count to at least thirty before I click on it, Dad's contact information will be there.

I get to thirty-two and let out my breath in a whoosh. When I click, the computer makes a beep-beep-beeping noise so loud I jump about a mile.

I reach for the speakers to turn the volume down but then realize it's not the computer at all. It's the smoke alarm in the kitchen. I left the pizza in the oven for way more than the eight minutes the box said it needed to cook.

I race into the smoky kitchen, turn off the oven and open it, which is the dumbest thing ever because even thicker blacker smoke pours out into my eyes. I turn away and cough. Then I pull up a chair to where the smoke alarm is on the ceiling by the hallway, grab a pile of papers from the table, jump up on the chair, and start fanning the smoke away from the smoke detector.

Finally, the beeping stops.

I climb down, put on an oven mitt, and take the pizza out of the oven. It looks like a melted hockey puck. I open the window and toss it out into the garden because it's still smoking. I try to fan more smoke out the window.

The one good thing is that Mrs. Delfino isn't upstairs to complain. Sorry—it's not good that she's dead, but she hated noise. She'd bang on the floor with her cane any time Mom played her music even a little too loud.

The smoke's starting to clear when there's a knock at the door.

A guy's holding open the screen door so he can knock on the glass. His face is pressed up close like he's looking in. He has gray hair and a mustache, and his cheeks are puffy and red, like he's been in the sun too much. He knocks again.

I unlock the door and open it a little. "Can I help you?"

"I'm Rudolph Delfino," he says, and steps into the house. "I'm Marietta's son and the executor of her will. I'm handling all her affairs." He looks around the kitchen and sniffs. "Did you have a fire here? What's going on? Where's your mother?"

"My pizza got overcooked. Mom's at work. She'll be back soon." I try to fan the smoke a little more with the papers I picked up from the table, but it doesn't help.

Rudolph Delfino takes the pile of papers from my hand and taps the letter on top. "I see she's received my letter," he says, and hands it back to me. "You tell her that my phone number is on there. I suggest she call me as soon as she gets home. I am not of the same mind-set as my mother when it comes to doing business."

He looks around the kitchen one more time and turns to go. "Put those papers where she'll see them." He slams the door so hard the glass rattles.

I stare down at the letter in my hand.

It's not written in Mrs. Delfino's curly old-lady writing. It's typed. And it's serious. Mrs. Delfino's son wants the rent from the last two months. He doesn't tell Mom to study hard, and he doesn't call her "dear."

My eyes skim to the last line of the letter.

If rent is not paid in full by October 1, eviction proceedings will begin immediately.

CHAPTER 12
Caches and Clues

I scrape peanut butter from an almost empty jar in the cupboard and spread it thin on a piece of bread. The pizza was probably freezer burned anyway.

I sit down at the kitchen table with my math homework and a sharp pencil. It's easy algebra, but I can't concentrate. The numbers in my brain are different.

Outgoing funds: Rent on the apartment—I think it's $800 a month—that hasn't been paid since August. School supplies. Groceries. Health insurance. Heating bills pretty soon. It's getting colder. Nursing school tuition.

Incoming funds: Nine bucks an hour and tips from one crummy waitressing job.

It doesn't matter how many extra shifts Mom gets. Nothing is going to make those numbers add up.

I shake my head and turn back to my homework. Except

there has to be something I'm missing here. As far as I know, this is the first time Mom's gotten so far behind on rent. Dad's been gone three years, and she's been doing nursing school and waitressing for two of them. How come there's suddenly not enough money when there was before?

I put my pencil down and check the clock. It should still be half an hour before Mom gets home.

I gather up the papers with Mr. Delfino's letter, open the door to Mom's room, and add the papers to the stack already on top of her dresser. The pile of bills is there, along with a folder of other papers and her checkbook on top.

We learned how to balance a checkbook in Home and Career Skills class last year. I turn to the front of it and check the withdrawals and deposits.

Most of it makes sense. Monthly checks to Mrs. Delfino until July. And then I can see why they stopped. There hasn't been $800 in the account since then.

I flip through the pages looking for what changed, and then I see it. A $900 deposit dated June first from Kirby Zigonski, Senior.

Child support. That's the other income that was paying the rent. And it hasn't shown up since the beginning of summer.

"Hi there!" When Mom gets home later, her voice has more energy than the rest of her. She sinks into a kitchen chair and sniffs the air. "Did you burn something?"

I close my binder, finally done with the math that should have taken ten minutes but took an hour. "Yeah, pizza."

"We have pizza?"

"We did. Till I burned it. I had a peanut butter sandwich instead."

"Here." She pulls a plastic to-go box out of her tote bag and hands it to me. I open it and find half a club sandwich, my favorite. "Here's a piece of pie, too." She hands me a smaller box.

"Awesome. Thanks." I take a big bite of the sandwich and figure I'll tell her about Rudolph Delfino tomorrow.

"So what did you do today?" Mom pulls a wad of ones from her pocket—tip money for the night—and heads for the office.

"Went out hiking with Gianna," I call in to her. "We messed around with the GPS unit. It's pretty cool."

"Is that what this stuff on the computer is all about?"

The big bite of pie I just took is suddenly sticky and dry in my mouth. The computer. I left Dad's profile page up on the screen when the smoke alarm went off.

"That's something Gianna was showing me with the geo-caching stuff. I didn't pay much attention."

"Well, finish up here while I get changed. Then I need to use the computer," Mom says. When I hear her bedroom door close, I race to the computer.

Geocaches. When the burned pizza alarm went off, I had just clicked on geocaches under Dad's profile. It's all loaded now. There's a list.

I can hear Mom's dresser drawers opening and closing. I scan the page quickly. There are two columns. One is a list of caches that Senior Searcher set up for other people to find. The other is a list of different people's caches that he found and logged.

I check the first list. Sure enough, there's the Nest Egg cache. And there are dates here, too. According to the log, Dad hid that one three years ago. It must have been right after he and Mom split up. No wonder he wanted to ditch the Canada key chain.

There are two more caches on the list, both set up around the same time. I need to find those. I wish it didn't get dark so fast after school in the fall.

I hear water run in the bathroom. Mom will be out soon. I click the back button and check the other list—geocaches that Dad has found.

This list is a lot longer. Dad must love geocaching. He's found forty-seven caches. I scan the list of dates. They start around the same time as the others—three years ago. But these dates are more spread out. Dad found caches in every season of the year—spring, summer, fall, and winter. I imagine him out in the woods freezing his butt off looking for some plastic container in the middle of February and it makes me laugh. It's totally like Dad to do something like that and refuse to give up.

The caches he found are listed in chronological order.

I scroll down and get to the last one just as Mom pops back into the room in her pajamas. "All right, off the computer," she says.

I quit the web browser and stand up. "I'm going to bed to read for a while."

"Not too late. You need to be up for school." Mom sinks into the chair and opens the folder of paperwork I saw on her dresser earlier. Rudolph's letter is right on top.

I get in bed with *Popular Mechanics*, but I stare past it at the ceiling, trying to make sense of the snapshots in my brain right now.

Rudolph's letter in Mom's folder.

Mom's checkbook with the dwindling balance.

Dad's last child support payment.

And his last geocache. Both dated June of this year. The same month I was supposed to see Dad for a summer camping trip. And he didn't make it.

What happened in June?

CHAPTER 13
Escape from In-School Suspension

"That must be when he moved in with her." Gianna brushes her curls out of her face, but the wind keeps blowing them back. Walking to school along the lake is great some mornings, but today it's cold and bitter and gray.

"With *who*?" I kick some leaves that have blown against the curb.

"I don't know who, but he must have moved in with someone, Zig. It makes sense."

"I think she's probably right," Ruby says quietly.

"Why wouldn't he tell me?"

"Well . . ." Gianna bites her lower lip, thinking. "Maybe she's a lot younger. And maybe he told her that *he's* really twenty-five, so he can't possibly have a twelve-year-old kid, and that's why he has to keep you a secret from her and her a secret from you."

Ruby picks up a chestnut and throws it at Gianna. "You've been watching too many soap operas with Nonna. Maybe he's nervous about telling you, Zig. Or he might be busy with work. Maybe he wants to wait until he can tell you in person."

"That's not good enough. I told you about the geocache log and the child support and stuff. It's been three months. He couldn't have called me or come to see me in three months?" I look at my watch. "Come on. We're going to be late."

Gianna hands me a horse chestnut as we start up the sidewalk to school. I whip it at the Ethan Allen Middle School sign and it makes a big loud *thwock* sound.

"Mr. Zigonski." Mr. Frankenbush is standing next to the sign, his arms crossed over his chest, which is the size of a school cafeteria garbage can. "You'll see me in my office immediately. We do not vandalize school property. And what if that had hit someone in the eye?"

This day keeps getting better and better.

I'm staring at the walls of a study carrel on three sides of me, concrete evidence that I'm a delinquent. But it's still hard to believe I've been assigned to the in-school suspension room for the crime of pegging one biodegradable horse chestnut at an indestructible wooden sign.

"Take out your homework," the monitor says.

"I finished it at home over the weekend," I tell her.

"Yeah, right," she says. "No kid in here has ever showed up with his work done. Take it out."

"Okay." Instead, I take out the list of GPS coordinates I printed before school this morning. The list from Dad's profile page.

"What's that?" The monitor frowns.

"Science," I say. I pull the GPS unit from my backpack, too. "We're learning latitude and longitude."

"Be quiet and get to work." She takes a loud slurp of coffee and disappears into her magazine. Perfect.

Within two hours, I've entered coordinates for all the new geocaches. I tuck the list and GPS unit into my backpack and pull out the math I did over the weekend. Might as well check it over.

"Back off, will ya? I'll find a seat myself!" Kevin Richards is pulling away from Mr. Teeter, the gym teacher.

"You'll sit where I tell you to sit." Teeter points to the desk next to mine. "Park it. And get some work out."

"I finished it all at home over the weekend," Richards says. I can't help the snort of laughter that comes out.

"What's your problem?" Then he sees it's me, and his eyes get wide. "Zigonski? What'd they put you in here for? Hack into the school computer system or something?"

I shake my head.

"No talking," says the monitor, not even looking up.

Mr. Teeter leaves, and I pretend to be busy with equations.

Richards leans over. "Seriously," he whispers. "What'd you do? Usually you have to punch somebody to get in here."

"Is that what you did?"

"Nah," he says, kicking his backpack. It's scuffed up with a few holes, like it's seen a lot of Kevin's boot. "I stole Ben Martin's sneakers outta the locker room."

"Why'd you do that?" I forget to whisper.

"No talking." The monitor turns a page in her magazine.

"I needed sneakers. You're pretty dumb for a smart kid." He looks down at my backpack. "You still got the alarm on that thing?"

I nod.

He nods back. "Probably a good call."

The monitor closes her magazine and stands up. "Time to go to the bathroom."

"I don't need to, thanks," I say.

"You've never been in here before, have you?" Kevin grins. "You have to go when they say you have to go."

We get marched down the hall to the boys' room and marched back. The ISS room is right next to the vice principal's office, which is right next to the eighth-grade entrance. I catch a glimpse of dark clouds through the hallway window before we're escorted back into our cell.

Every time I reach into my backpack to get another already-finished assignment so I can pretend to work on it, my fingers brush the GPS unit. Every time that happens, my brain runs through the cache names I entered. Skywalker Stretch. Super-hero's Lair. Tabletop Treasure. That one's right behind the school, not far from the cache Gianna and I found yesterday.

The monitor is knitting now. She hasn't looked up in half an hour.

I reach for my social studies book and touch the GPS again. I take it out and press the on button, but you can't get a clear signal in a building like this. If I were closer to a window, it might work. Or if I took it outside.

I take out my social studies homework and pretend to check over the crossword puzzle I filled in over the weekend. A big hand snatches the paper off my desk.

Kevin puts his finger to his lips. "No talking in ISS," he says, and starts copying my answers onto his blank crossword.

"Give that back!" I whisper.

"Mr. Zigonski!" The monitor glares at me. "How many times do I have to speak with you about the rules? You are not doing anything to improve your situation today."

She looks at me as if she's waiting for me to say I'm sorry.

Sorry for what? For committing the terrible crime of throwing an acorn? For having done my homework before I got to school? For not rolling over while this jerk steals my homework?

Nope. Not sorry for any of those things.

I have to clench my teeth together to keep from saying what I really think. It feels like my heart is about to explode out of my chest.

I cannot stay here all afternoon. Not in this chair. Not in this room. Not in this stupid school.

I'm lucky I even made it to lunchtime.

The monitor walks us to the end of the cafeteria line and glances over at the faculty lunchroom. "I'll be right back," she says. "If you get through the line before then, return to the ISS room on your own."

I go through the line.

I pick up a milk from the cooler.

I hand my tray to the cafeteria ladies so they can serve up my sandwich.

I say please. I say thank you.

I'm through the line before the monitor gets back, so I return to the ISS room.

I put down my tray, pick up my backpack, and head for the door.

"Hey!" Kevin says, walking back in with his double order of grilled cheese. "Where you going?"

"I forgot to get a napkin," I tell him.

I walk out of the room, right out the door to the street.

CHAPTER 14
A Soggy Search

When I step outside, the wind feels like a splash of cold water in my face. I take off running toward the path that winds through the woods. Best to get out of sight before the monitor gets back.

I should be looking over my shoulder. I should feel nervous about leaving without permission. I should be scared I'll get caught. But you know what? I don't care. It feels good to be out.

When I can't see the brick of the school building through the trees anymore, I stop and pull the GPS from my backpack.

I turn it on and wait for it to find the satellites. Then I press the button to select the page for Dad's new geocache, Tabletop Treasure.

The GPS says I should go 0.57 miles south-southeast, which is weird. I'm pretty sure the river is closer than half a mile. Leave it to Dad to hide a geocache underwater.

I have to leave the path right away, which is probably good. I wouldn't be surprised if Mr. Frankenbush walks the nature trail at lunchtime, hunting for kids skipping class.

A thorn bush catches my sleeve and leaves a big scratch on my arm. I smear away the blood with my other sleeve and keep walking. Just like last time, the GPS unit switches from miles to yards as I get closer. The trees thin out, and when the GPS says I'm 200 yards from the cache, I can see the river.

I keep walking and watch the numbers go down.

142 yards.

120 yards.

I have to loop around a big marshy spot so I don't get my feet soaking wet, but when I get back on the path, I'm even closer.

72 yards.

45 yards.

When the GPS unit says I'm 18 yards from Dad's geocache, I'm standing in tall, rustly cattails, right at the river's edge. I can't keep going. My sneakers are already sinking into the mud. A few more steps and I'll be in running water.

I try walking up and down the riverbank, to see if the coordinates are off, but every time I turn, that stupid arrow turns, too. It points back at the middle of the river, where there's nothing but cold, rushing water.

Nice, Dad. Make a promise and don't deliver on it.

Again.

I'm about to turn back when a heron flies right over my head. Its wingspan is huge, maybe six feet. Ruby would love it. The bird soars with its toes pointed behind it, all the way across the river. Then it circles partway back and lands upstream on a tiny island I hadn't noticed before.

The heron stands tall and looks down its long beak into the water. Then it blasts into the weeds with that beak and comes up with a fish, flopping back and forth. It spreads its wings and pumps them to take off again, downstream toward the lake.

My stomach grumbles. I should have eaten my sandwich before I left. Even raw fish is starting to look good.

I start to turn around and then realize that the arrow is pointing straight at the heron's island. Great thinking, Dad. Everyone brings a small watercraft along when they go geocaching. No problem.

We've had a ton of rain this fall. The river's running too fast and high for me to even think about wading out to the island. Instead, I walk along shore to get closer.

Not far from where the bird caught its lunch, a rotten tree stretches from the bank almost all the way out to that little island. I step up onto the part of the tree that's resting on the rocks and bounce a little.

It feels solid enough. And now I can see that it ends about three feet from where the rocks of the island begin. An easy jump.

I set down my backpack in case I end up getting wet. No sense in wrecking my homework and the GPS unit if I go in.

It's easy to walk one foot in front of the other along the tree. I'm about halfway across when I take a step and the log dips into the water. Cold river water sloshes over my sneaker.

I'm still too far from the island to jump, so I step forward again. The log dips lower, but only a little. I take another step and it holds. Another. And another.

But then I slip on the rotten wood. My feet slide out from under me. The log catches me across my left shoulder blade so hard I can barely breathe, and I fall in. Icy water shocks my whole body.

I grab on to the log with both arms and hold tight as the current tries to sweep the rest of me down the river. I cling to the old tree and catch my breath until I can pull myself back on top to sit. Finally, I get my feet back under me and stand up.

My jeans feel like they weigh a thousand pounds as I take the last tiny steps toward the island. When I get to the end of the log, I can see bottom. It's not like I can get any wetter, so I step into the water and slosh to shore.

The GPS unit is back on the other side of the water, so I have no idea which direction I should be looking for Tabletop Treasure. The weeds are tall and tangled. I keep tripping on roots, and my legs are so cold I can't feel them anymore.

I step through a thicket into a small clearing, a spot where the weeds aren't so high. And there it is—a rock formation that looks exactly like somebody's dining room table. It's a small block of rock, maybe two feet wide and four feet long, with a much bigger rock slab balanced on top of it. If you pulled up a chair, it would be the greatest picnic spot ever.

I step up and run my hand over the smooth rock tabletop. Dad wouldn't leave the cache right on top, so where could it be? I poke through the weeds under the table to see if there's any Tupperware stashed there.

Nope.

I walk in a circle, all around the table. Nothing.

I pull myself up onto the tabletop and flop down to look up at the clouds.

My mood is grayer than they are. I'm sopping wet, freezing, and hungry. I didn't find the cache, and now I have to get back across the stupid, slippery tree somehow.

Kevin was right. For a guy who's supposed to be so smart, I'm pretty dumb.

I don't even want to think about the trouble I'm in for walking out of ISS. They've probably already called Mom at work.

I slip my hand under the edge of the table so I can pull myself up and get going, but I don't feel the hard, flat rock I'm expecting.

I feel something round. Cylindrical.

I climb down and squat to look up at the underside of the rock. A film canister is duct-taped there. My heart races as I work the tape loose and pry the lid off the container.

I found it.

Rolled up in Dad's film container is a cache log with a little pencil, a Vermont state quarter, and a bookmark-sized scrap of paper with a quote written on it.

> *Everything that is done in the world is done by hope.*
> —Martin Luther

CHAPTER 15
Soggy Sneakers

"Okay, please do, and if you hear anything—" Mom stops mid-sentence when I walk into the house. "Actually, he just came in. Yes, he's fine. Thanks . . . Okay . . . Goodbye."

She slams the phone onto the counter with a *ka-thunk* and looks at me. "I do not know *what* you could have been thinking." She's leaning on the counter in her diner outfit with the checked red-and-white skirt, her apron with her order pad and pencil still sticking up from the pocket. She must have raced out of work.

I stand by the door, dripping. I don't know what I could have been thinking either.

"Do you have any idea what this afternoon has been like?" Mom goes on. "First, I get a call saying that you defaced school property. They go on to tell me that not only were you sent to in-school suspension for the day, but that you then proceeded to walk out of the building and disappear. That was three *hours* ago. Where have you been?"

What can I say? Nothing. That's what.

I can't tell her that chucking one dumb chestnut at a sign isn't "defacing school property." I can't tell her about that ogre Kevin showing up to be my neighbor in the ISS room. And I sure can't tell her about looking for Dad.

"It was stupid," I finally say.

"I know *that*. I asked where you were."

"The woods."

She looks down at my sopping sneakers, the dripping cuffs of my jeans, the puddle of muddy water growing on the kitchen floor.

"And the river. I kind of fell in."

She shakes her head and looks as me as if I still haven't answered her question. But she asked where. Not why. I told the truth. I fold my arms and stare back.

After a minute, she sighs, turns to get a glass from the cupboard, and fills it with water. She takes a drink, then another deep breath. Her voice is softer this time, like she's afraid I might run out of here, too.

"Kirb, what were you *doing*?"

I shake my head. "Just thinking. It's been a crummy week, and I needed to get away. Haven't you ever felt that way?"

Now Mom looks like she's going to cry. She blinks fast and

rubs her hands on her apron. "I have to get back," she says. "Clean up this mess. Stay home."

"I will."

She leans in to give me a quick hug and leaves.

I change into dry clothes and mop up the river water. I *should* be her responsible kid and do homework now.

But I don't feel like it. I can't concentrate.

Everywhere I go feels like the wrong place. The kitchen table. The computer desk. The sofa.

Even my bedroom. Usually, it's my favorite place in the world. I've got posters of Nikola Tesla and Ada Lovelace on the wall. Last year's science project—a model hydrogen car— takes up half my bookshelf. My favorite LEGO creation takes up the other half. I made it when I was ten, using the parts from five of those sets that tell you exactly what to build and how to build it. I never built the space shuttle or the working dump truck or the knight's castle, but I made a killer city-of-the-future with the parts. I even wired the whole thing so the little LEGO townspeople would have power.

Tonight, I don't even feel like turning on the streetlights.

I wander down to the computer and log on to the geocaching site.

Senior Searcher hasn't posted anything new.

I pull the paper with the quote from my pocket. It's already so crumpled it feels soft in my hand, like cloth instead of paper.

> *Everything that is done in the world is done by hope.*
> *—Martin Luther*

Except the things that are done out of stupidity.

The computer dings at me. I set the paper beside it and see a message from Gianna.

MapleGrl: hey
CircuitBoy: Hi.
MapleGrl: hey you're there!!! where'd you go?
frankenbush sent out the cops
CircuitBoy: I was protesting. I was wrongly accused,
and then Kevin Richards got thrown in ISS with me.
So I left.
MapleGrl: seriously?
CircuitBoy: Yeah. Mom was beyond mad.
MapleGrl: r u grounded?
CircuitBoy: No. But only because I think she forgot.
She had to get back to work.
MapleGrl: so where were you?
CircuitBoy: In the woods behind school. Geocaching.

I wait and listen to the clock on the wall tick. MapleGrl doesn't type anything else.

CircuitBoy: You still there?
MapleGrl: Yep.

CircuitBoy: How come you're not typing?

MapleGrl: Just thinking.

CircuitBoy: ??????

MapleGrl: About your dad.

CircuitBoy: Gee, it's him. I know it's him. I need to track down the rest of the geocaches to find out where he is. There must be information somewhere.

MapleGrl: Okay.

CircuitBoy: Okay, what?

MapleGrl: I'll help. I bet Ruby will, too.

I lean down to unzip my backpack, pull out the GPS unit, and turn it on. I have the coordinates for three more caches that he found. Two are pretty close.

CircuitBoy: Tomorrow after school?

MapleGrl: u got it

I look down at the coordinates on the GPS unit again. The next set of coordinates looks like it might be close to the river, too.

CircuitBoy: One more thing.

MapleGrl: ???

CircuitBoy: Wear boots.

MapleGrl: u r so weird

CircuitBoy: See you tomorrow!

MapleGrl: L8R G8R

I shut down the computer and tuck the GPS unit back in my bag with an extra set of batteries. Part of me is glad Gee's coming tomorrow, but part of me feels annoyed, like this should just be my adventure and Dad's. Even though he's not along for it.

I pick up the quote from the film container, rub my thumb against the soft wrinkled paper, and wonder what Dad left in the next cache.

CHAPTER 16
Follow the Arrow

Ruby's in the front hallway taping up posters when we get to school.

SAVE ROOKERY BAY!

Underneath, someone's done this incredible drawing of a great blue heron standing in reeds with a fish in its mouth. I tap the heron's beak with my finger. "Is this yours?" I ask Gianna. She's a great artist.

She nods. "Ruby wanted something to catch people's attention. We're going to try and get a crowd at the city council meeting."

"You think kids will actually show up?" I look around at my fellow eighth graders and wonder about their sense of civic responsibility. Walker Tate and Spencer McMahon are tossing a

Frisbee back and forth, up and down the hall. Mary Beth Rot-willer is taping up sparkle letters in her locker. Bianca Rinaldi is showing Kevin Richards one of the moves she learned in her hip-hop dance class over the weekend. She looks like a bird I saw doing a mating dance on the Discovery Channel once.

"Extra credit." Gianna smiles. "Ruby convinced the teachers to offer social studies points to anybody who shows up."

"Caring about your environment and taking part in the dem-ocratic process is a citizenship issue," Ruby says, taping up a poster. "Here." She hands me another one while she picks at the edge of the Scotch tape with her fingernail. I turn it over. This one says: HERONS ARE HOMEOWNERS, TOO.

"After school, we need to put some up downtown," she says.

"After school, I have other plans." Thankfully, I ended up getting lunch detention instead of after-school punishment for walking out the other day, so our geocaching plans are safe. I turn to Gianna. "And you have plans, too. Right?"

Gianna nods. "But we can do both. We'll help Ruby with the posters, and then we'll all check out another geocache."

The bell rings.

"Shoot!" Gianna starts digging in her backpack. ChapStick, an empty water bottle, four colored pencils, and half a granola bar fall out. "I think my science homework is still in my locker. I'll see you later!"

"Later" turns into a whole lot later when Gianna has to stay after school to redo the science homework she never found. It's almost four by the time we pass the public library and turn the corner for downtown.

I see Mom's car outside the diner. "Want to put a poster up here?"

"Sure." Ruby pulls open the door and the pancake smell makes me wish we were here for snacks and homework instead of a publicity mission.

"Better check with Alan." I nod toward the cash register, where he's pulling on his mustache and frowning at the machine. Ruby and Gianna walk over, and I pull out the GPS while they talk.

"We're hoping we could put up a poster about the Smugglers Island condo project," Gianna says.

Alan smiles at her. "Shopping for condos, are you?"

"No!" Ruby almost shouts, then tones it down. "I mean, we don't support that project. It would have a terrible impact on the great blue herons that nest there."

Alan nods. "You can put your poster up by the counter." He looks at it more closely. "I might have to stop by that meeting. Thank you for bringing it to my attention."

"We have to go," I say, nudging Ruby and Gianna toward the door. Mom gives a quick wave from the counter, where she's pouring coffee.

"I bet Mr. Mulcahy will let us put one at the CornerMart,"

Gianna says as we leave the diner. I start to follow her, but the
arrow on the GPS unit is pointing the other way. While we were
in the diner, I called up Dad's cache called Superhero's Lair.

"Hey, guys . . ." I stop and look down at the small screen in
my hand. "I know we have more posters, but we're really close
to this Superhero's Lair cache. If we go up to the store, we'll be
walking the opposite way. Can we check this out first?"

"Sure. Hold still a second." Ruby rolls up the three posters
we have left and puts them in my backpack. They're sticking out
the top, but it's better than carrying them. "Okay, remind me
how this works."

"It's sort of like a little god," Gianna says. "Oh great and
almighty small yellow plastic device!" She takes it from me
and holds it up to the sun. "Hear our wishes and point your
little arrow where the geocache is!" She brings it down and
shows Ruby. "See? We have to go that way."

Forty minutes later, we've walked up and down Bridge Street
five times, and the GPS unit keeps telling us the same thing.

Out there.

Out there, as in, out on the lake.

"Maybe there's something wrong with it," Ruby says, squint-
ing at the screen for the fiftieth time.

"Maybe there's something wrong with him," I say.

"Who?"

"His dad," Gianna says. "Zig thinks his dad has been to this geocache." She explains how I went online, how the name Senior Searcher convinced me that the profile belonged to Dad. The way she says it makes me a little mad. Always "Zig thinks" and "Zig believes," like she doesn't think it's true.

We start back toward the diner. The GPS unit points left. Out to the open lake.

"I guess we're not going to get this one," I say finally.

Gianna leans in to look at the GPS screen again. She's so close her hair tickles my neck. It smells like apples.

"Point three seven miles," she says. "That's like a third of a mile that way." She points out over the lake, right at Smugglers Island. "Zig! I bet it's on the island!"

"My aunt lives near here," Ruby says. "She's been out there; it's only about a quarter mile offshore."

"Only a quarter of a mile? Let's swim it right now." I'm being sarcastic and rotten, but I can't help it. Every time I think I'm going to learn something about Dad, I end up with a big fat nothing.

"The water's pretty cold now. Anybody got wet suits?" Gianna jokes.

"No." Ruby taps her index finger against her bottom lip. "But I know where we can borrow a boat."

CHAPTER 17
The Search for Superhero's Lair

"Are you sure it's not too rough? These waves are huge. Did anybody even check the forecast? Maybe we should do this another day." Five minutes in a kayak, and I think I'm going to be seasick. Lakesick. Whatever.

Gianna sits behind me in the double red kayak we borrowed from Ruby's aunt, while Ruby paddles next to us in the green single. We're headed out to Smugglers Island.

"You've got a life vest, Zig. It's fine." Ruby laughs and splashes us with her paddle. "My aunt never would have let us take the boats if it was going to get rougher."

"Besides," Gianna says. "These are really stable." She tips back and forth to prove it. My lunch flops around in my stomach.

"What's the GPS say?" Ruby calls over.

"Point one eight miles that way." I motion toward the island. "It must be around on the other side."

Ruby nods. "We'll paddle around."

"Can't we land here and walk across?" I'm desperate to have earth under my feet.

Ruby shakes her head. "Poison ivy. The interior of the island is loaded with it."

"I bet the smugglers planted it years and years ago," Gianna says. "So no one would disturb their treasure chests while they were off at sea."

"Nah," Ruby says. "The smugglers this island is named after weren't smuggling gold and jewels. My aunt told me they were running booze during the Prohibition era. She's found some old empty bottles diving off shore at her camp."

When we paddle around to the other side of the island, the wind is blocked by a peninsula, and the water finally settles down. Here, the surface barely has a ripple. It's hard to believe it's the same lake.

"Now what's it say?" Ruby waits for me to check the GPS unit.

"Forty-two yards. This way." I point at the island, to a spot where a ten- or twelve-foot cliff drops right into the water.

"We can't land there." Ruby pulls her kayak up alongside ours. Gianna reaches out and grabs Ruby's boat so she doesn't drift away. Two seagulls sit on the very tip of the rocky peninsula, cawing at us.

"Can I see that?" Ruby takes the GPS from me and frowns at it. "It's definitely pointing at the cliff. Maybe we can land someplace else and hike to that spot."

"What about the poison ivy?" Gianna wrinkles her nose, and the freckles on it smush together.

"Yeah, that's going to be a problem." Ruby sighs. She shakes the GPS unit a little, like it might change its mind. The wind has picked up, even on this side of the island, and we've drifted closer to shore.

"What's it say now?" I ask.

"Here." Ruby hands the GPS back so I can check the distance. It's still pointing at that same rocky drop-off, but this time the number is way down.

"Seventy-nine feet." I stare at the cliffs. They look like they're about seventy-nine feet from us now. "The geocache has to be right near shore. Actually . . . look!" I point to shore, my finger following the line of the GPS unit's arrow. "See how some rocks are worn away near the water line?"

"Probably from waves," Ruby says. "Sometimes the lake is a lot higher."

"It's made all these little caves." I paddle closer. "I bet this is where he hid the geocache!" I grab a rock edge that leads into the biggest cave and hold us there. "A person would fit in here; it only gets narrow at the very top. And look!" I hold up the GPS unit. "It says we're three feet from our target, and the arrow points right into this cave. How deep's the water?"

Ruby bumps into us with her kayak. She pulls a small lake chart out of the dry hatch, unrolls it, and frowns. "Over your head. And the kayaks are too wide to fit. We'll have to come back this summer when the water's lower. By the middle of July, it should be easier to—"

"I'm going in." I've already tightened the straps on my life jacket. I lean down to untie my sneakers but then think better of it and leave them on.

"You're nuts," Gianna says. "It's almost October, Zig. That water's cold."

"It's fine. And I'll float." I know the water's cold, but the GPS keeps pointing into that cave. It might as well be saying it out loud. *Dad . . . Dad . . . Dad . . .*

I tighten the life vest one more time and try to figure out how I can get into the water without tipping Gee in with me. Finally, I convince Ruby to hold the kayak steady while I balance over my seat and flip my legs off one side.

When I go in, it feels like I've plunged into a giant glass of ice water.

"Is it cold?" Gianna asks.

I nod. So cold I can't talk. Or breathe, really.

My legs prickle with icy needles for a minute but get numb pretty quickly. I kick my way toward the cave, but waves keep coming at me, floating me up and away from where I need to be.

Finally, I make my way to the opening in the rocks and stand up. It's not as deep here—only about three feet, so I can touch bottom. I put my hands on the edges of the rock walls to steady myself. It's slippery, covered in cold algae. My fingers are numb.

I step into the crevice as a big wave sloshes in. The cave narrows quickly as I move toward the back. My shoulders brush the rocky walls as I walk, but so far my head is clear.

I thought the light from outside would reach to the back wall, but it doesn't. Even though my eyes have had time to adjust, I can't see ahead of me. There's a big wave, a hollow schlooping noise. Then a squeak that doesn't fit in with the water sounds.

"Hey!" I call to the kayaks floating outside the entrance. "Did you hear that?"

"The water? It sounds cool, doesn't it?" Gianna ducks down to look in the cave. "Can you see in there?"

Before I can answer, there's another squeaking sound. A lot of squeaking sounds, right over my head.

"Ruby, can you aim that flashlight in here?"

Just as the beam finds the back of the cave, the squeaking sounds explode into a collective fluttering screech. Bats!

"Gahh!" Wings beat against my face and flap in my hair. I splash out of the cave, and the bats swarm out around me.

They disappear around a curve in the cliff—probably into some other cave where no stupid kids decided to go swimming.

I catch my breath and find Ruby and Gianna. They hurried away from the cave entrance when the bats showed up, but now Gianna paddles back and looks down at me, bobbing on the waves. "Eww. You've got bat poop in your hair."

"It's actually called guano," Ruby says, as if that might make me feel better. "Here." She pulls up alongside Gianna and steadies the double kayak so I can climb in. "We better head back to Aunt Barbara's place."

We paddle without talking for a while. Then Gianna starts giggling. "It *was* called Superhero's Lair, you know. *Bat*man, get it? You can't say nobody warned you."

Ruby's aunt Barbara is waiting on shore when we pull up in the kayaks. She was worried because the wind was picking up. She steps into the water and pulls the boats onto the sand. She takes one look at my wet clothes and bat-guano hair and sends me inside to take a shower.

When I get out, she's standing at the door with her purse over her shoulder and her car keys in her hand.

"The girls told me what happened with the bats. Ready for your rabies shot?"

My mother meets us at the doctor's office, still in her apron from Alan's.

I rush up to her. "Mom, I don't need shots. It's not like I got bit or anything."

"Sit down." Aunt Barbara points me to the chair between Ruby and Gianna, and I sit. "They need your insurance card, Laurie."

Mom looks at the receptionist behind the desk and then back at Ruby's aunt.

"Your insurance card," she says again.

Mom opens her purse and starts poking through it, but it looks more like she's stirring things around than looking for anything. Finally, she says, "I'll have to bring it in later." She sits down at the desk to fill out paperwork.

"I guess maybe that wasn't the best idea today, huh?" Ruby pulls out the GPS unit and clicks through the coordinates for the different caches.

"I still don't see how he could have hidden the cache in there with all the bats," Gianna says. "But it was the only cave big enough for a person to fit."

I nod. "It must have been back there somewhere. Maybe it was wedged in a crack along the ceiling or something. I should have had the light the whole time, I guess."

"We should have checked the clue, too." Gianna pulls a computer printout from her backpack. "I printed it last night but forgot about it."

I hold the page in my hands and look down.

QR URELQ LQ WKLV FDYH, EXW BRX'OO ILQG SOHQWB RI EDWV!

ABCDEFGHIJKLMNOPQRSTUVWXYZ
DEFGHIJKLMNOPQRSTUVWXYZABC

My hair drips onto the puzzle. "Got a pencil?"

Gianna hands me one, and I get to work on the cipher. Dad used the same code for all his caches, so it's not too tough. I figure it out, letter by letter. If today had been any kind of different day, if this week hadn't been so awful, if things weren't so crummy, I probably would have laughed.

Instead, I stare at it as the nurse calls my name.

"Kirby Zigonski? Time for the first of your seven shots."

"Here." I hand it to Gianna on my way through the white door. "Another message from Dad. He always was a funny guy."

ABCDEFGHIJKLMNOPQRSTUVWXYZ
DEFGHIJKLMNOPQRSTUVWXYZABC

QR URELQ LQ WKLV FDYH, EXW BRX'OO ILQG
SOHQWB RI EDWV!

NO ROBIN IN THIS CAVE, BUT YOU'LL FIND
PLENTY OF BATS!

CHAPTER 18
Dances and Deadlines

"Hey, bat boy!" Kevin Richards shouts from the top step of the school entrance. He drops his backpack so he can flap his arms up and down.

I hold the door for Gianna and Ruby. "How'd he get hold of that one so fast?"

"Remember the doctor's office receptionist?" Ruby says.

"Yeah."

"Mrs. Richards."

Really, can this day get worse? I woke up this morning freezing because I left my window cracked open last night. I couldn't find socks without holes. And I couldn't stop thinking about what day it was. October first. The date on the letter. The "or else" date.

When I got up this morning, Mom was sitting at the table

surrounded by papers and envelopes, scribbling in her check-book. She looked like she'd been up all night.

She offered to fix me breakfast. I didn't want to tell her we've been out of cereal for two days, so I said, "Nah, I'll grab something at school."

I didn't. Now my stomach feels hollow, and the rest of me is all shaky.

"Good morning, boys and girls!" Our principal, Ms. Hemp-stead, used to teach elementary school and starts the morning announcements every day as if we're all six years old. "It's a lovely day outside, and we have some important news from the student council. There will be a school dance on November first. And checking our calendar today . . . it's October first."

No kidding.

I open my locker, lean in to get my computer class folder, and hear Kevin Richards laugh as a giant hand shoves me between the shoulders.

My head catches the edge of the locker, but what's worse is the pain in my arm when I slam it into the locker door try-ing to catch myself. It gets me right where I had the shot yes-terday. And I have to go back for another one tomorrow and three more after that. I'm going to be seeing a lot of Kevin's mom.

Kevin saunters down the hall to gym class at the other end of the building. I imagine myself chasing him down the hallway and tackling him to the floor. Then I have a better idea.

Mr. Teeter always makes us run laps if we're late. I call down the hall.

"Hey, Richards!"

He turns and stops, surprised that the meek and bruised Kirby Zigonski has spoken to him. "Yeah?"

"Did you finish that crossword puzzle you were working on the other day?"

"What's it to you?" He sneers at me but doesn't leave.

"I'm genuinely concerned about your academics," I say. "You know, poor achievement in middle school is considered a key indicator when it comes to the likelihood of future incarceration."

"What're you talkin' about?"

"Oh, never mind, I guess." I count down with the second hand on my watch. "I better get going."

Science class is right next to my locker, and I step in just as the bell rings. Mrs. Loring starts to close the door but not before I hear Kevin swear from all the way down the hallway.

He really hates running laps.

The mental picture of Richards running in circles makes me feel a little better. So does our science lesson—a lab on pulse and exercise where we get to use special probes to measure one another's heart rates. The equipment feeds the data into a laptop computer Mrs. Loring has set up and graphs it so you can see changes.

"Want to go first?" I ask Gianna. She and Ruby and I always try to work together. Today, we're in groups of four. Mrs. Loring put Robert Rensliver with us because he didn't have a partner. Ruby's telling him all about Birds First, hoping for a new recruit to show up at the next city council meeting.

Gee and I start to get the lab set up.

"Okay—how's it work again?" Gianna holds the wires and looks up at me.

"You have to clip it on your belt," I say. "Here." I lean over with the clip end of the probe to help her before I realize she's not wearing a belt and her shirt—this fluffy, ruffly thing—ends right at the top of her pants. I reach over to clip on the probe without touching her, but she erupts into a fit of giggles and doubles over.

"Zig, that tickles!"

"I didn't touch you." My face is hot. I turn to Ruby. "I didn't even get close to her, and she started laughing, I swear."

Ruby's grinning the way Nonna does when she teases Gianna and me about us getting married someday. Nonna does that pretty much whenever she remembers who I am. Ruby holds out her hand for the probe. "Maybe I better help her."

No argument here.

Gianna keeps glancing over at me. Her face is red, too. Maybe it's because of the exercise. Although someone who runs three miles every morning isn't likely to be flushed and winded over twenty jumping jacks for an experiment.

Gianna acts weird at lunch, too. She sits by me—she always does that, so that's not the weird part—and she keeps looking over with her mouth open like she's going to say something. But she never does.

"What?" I finally ask Gianna when Ruby gets up to recruit more kids for her city council meeting.

"Huh?" she says.

"You keep almost saying something."

"How do you know what I'm almost saying?" Her cheeks flush again.

"I don't. That's why I'm asking you what you keep almost saying."

"Maybe I'm not almost saying anything," she says.

"Okay." I put away my peanut butter sandwich and pull out an apple.

"Hmph," she says. I pretend not to hear. She'll just say she didn't say it anyway.

I take a bite of my apple and look out the window. It's getting cloudy.

"Hmph," Gianna says again.

I turn back to her. "Hmph?"

She sighs. "Never mind."

"Okay." I take another bite of the apple.

Gianna takes a deep breath and spits out, "You-know-there's-a-dance-next-month-right-because-I'm-thinking-about-going-and-I-was-wondering-if-you-think-you'll-probably-think-about-going-even-though-dances-are-kind-of-dumb-and-not-your-thing-I-still-wondered-if-you-thought-you-might." She bites her lip and looks at me. I have a mouth full of apple.

"Or not," she says, and starts to stand up with her tray.

I swallow fast. "No, hold on," I say. She sits back down. "I . . . uh . . ." Did she just ask me to the dance? No, she definitely didn't do that. Gee doesn't even like dances, I don't think. At least she didn't used to like them.

"It's okay if you don't want to go." She looks disappointed.

"No, I'll probably go."

"You will?" She looks surprised.

Actually, I'm surprised, too. "I mean . . . well . . . I could go. I'm not really sure it'd be the greatest or anything, but if you think it would be fun and you and Ruby are going, then I guess I could go. If you want."

She nods and stands up. "They usually have Rice Krispies Treats at the snack table," she says, like that clinches it.

And I have to be honest. It kind of does.

I have another bite of my apple and watch the milk truck guy wheel in a crate of cartons.

Gianna wants me to go to that dance. And I actually want to go. How about that?

The warning bell rings, so I toss my apple core and grab my books. My feet carry me to social studies, where my eyes stay focused on the movie about the civil rights movement, but my brain keep bouncing back to Gianna and the dance.

And Rice Krispies Treats. Lunch feels like a long time ago.

Finally, the last bell rings. Ruby has some meeting, and Gee has cross-country practice, so I walk home on my own. My arm hurts a little, but the rest of me feels great. I unzip my jacket.

"Hello there, young man!" Mr. Webster's coming down the steps of the library. I wave like I used to when I'd see him out for his walk when I was delivering papers.

A warm wind plays around with the leaves that have fallen, whipping them into miniature tornadoes. I pick up a red one.

I don't even remember that today is October first—the "or else" date.

Until I get home.

CHAPTER 19
Goodbye, Yellow Curtains

Mom is on the phone when I get home. Her face is red.

"Beck, I don't know. I don't *know*." She must be talking to Aunt Becka, which is weird. Even though they only live a few blocks away, she and Mom don't talk much.

Mom sighs hard. "Well, no. I mean, I'm not sure. This all just happened. The letter says we have until the seventh, but I want to take care of this now and find a new—" She stops mid-sentence when she sees me.

"Hey, Mom." She doesn't say hi. She just looks at me. Then I guess she remembers she has the phone in her hand.

"Sorry. Yeah, he just got home," she says into the phone. "No. He doesn't." Another sigh. "Well, now. Obviously. I don't have much choice, do I?" Long pause. Quieter sigh. "I know . . . I know. Sorry. And thanks. We'll see you tomorrow night."

Mom puts the phone back on the hook but doesn't turn around. She tips her head up and looks at the ceiling like she left something up there. I look up, too, but all I see are cobwebs in the corner, a little smoky looking. Probably from the day I burned the pizza.

Mom finally turns to the cupboard, gets two glasses, and clinks them full of ice cubes. She fills them with water and slides one across the table. "Sit down, okay?"

I sit. I drink my water, even though I'm not thirsty. And I wait.

"We're going to be staying with Aunt Becka for a while," Mom says. She takes a drink of her water. I wait for her to say more. She doesn't.

"But we don't like Aunt Becka," I say finally. That totally came out wrong. And even though Aunt Becka irritates Mom, she'd never admit that. "I mean . . ."

"Aunt Becka is doing us a huge favor," Mom says. "She's letting us crash in her guest room for now. We're going to look for a new apartment."

"When?"

"We're moving tomorrow."

"Tomorrow! We can't move tomorrow."

"It's what we're doing, Kirb." She takes my almost-full water glass and dumps the rest in the sink. The ice sounds like glass breaking on metal. Like my life smashing into pieces here at the kitchen table. Mom's overreacting.

I decide to tell her I know. "Mom, I saw the letter from Mrs. Delfino's son. But he can't just throw us out because you missed a month or two of rent. Isn't there—"

"*Three* months. I missed three months." She shoves the glass into the dishwasher. This time, the sound of glass breaking is real.

Mom swears and reaches in for the broken glass, then pulls her hand back fast, like something bit her. Drops of blood drip onto the dirty knives and forks.

"Mom." I jump up, rip off two paper towels, and hand them to her. "Here."

Her eyes are wet. She's holding her breath, trying not to cry.

"Mom, listen. Just call Dad. He'll figure this out. He can—"

"That is *not* an option." Mom's voice is sharper than the glass.

"Okay, fine. But . . . don't people have to go to court or something to throw you out of your apartment?"

"He did that a month ago." Mom picks up a manila folder from the table and waves it at me. "He'd been advising his mother on her finances and saw that rent wasn't being paid on time. Marietta was wonderful about it. She so wanted me to get this nursing degree. But he filed the papers for her anyway."

I reach for the folder. At first, Mom shakes her head. Then she half laughs, half sighs and hands it to me.

I skim the papers inside. Most of it's legal stuff I don't understand. My eyes stop on the line that gives us a deadline.

Thirty days.

Thirty days from the date of the court document.

And there it is on the top of the paper. September 3. Two days after last month's rent didn't show up.

"So we have until Saturday? That's it?" The folder shakes in my hand. I look around the kitchen. At the gauzy yellow curtains Mom brought from the old apartment where she and Dad lived when they first got married. At my last science test taped to our loud, old refrigerator. At the clay handprint on the window-sill. I made it for Mother's Day in second grade. I can't believe she kept it there so long. I look at the blue glass vase I got Mom at a yard sale last summer. She loves the way the sun shines through it and makes blue shapes on the table. It's full of little purple flowers—the only ones still blooming in her garden out front.

Her garden that won't be her garden for much longer.

"We have until Saturday, but I'm working double shifts at the end of the week, so we need to move our stuff tomorrow." She picks up her purse and starts rummaging in it.

"Mom, I can't—I have a social studies test tomorrow. And a science chapter to read. And I've got math and—"

She whirls around with her truck keys in her hand. "Has it occurred to you that this might be inconvenient for me, too? I can't have you acting like a six-year-old right now. I can't. Go do your homework. I'm going to the store to get boxes."

She lets the screen door slam behind her. She hates it when

the screen door slams. I guess since we won't be living here anymore, it doesn't matter.

I walk to the door and watch her get in the white pickup truck Dad left with us. The driver's door doesn't open right anymore, so Mom has to get in the passenger side and slide over on the seat. I press my forehead against the cool glass, watch her put the keys in the ignition, wait for the truck to back out of the driveway.

It doesn't.

Mom sits there, her arms folded in front of her over the steering wheel, her head down, her shoulders shaking.

After a while—maybe five or ten minutes—the truck backs out of the driveway. Slow. Like the way you'd pull a splinter out of your hand little by little so it won't hurt.

And then it does anyway.

CHAPTER 20
Home Sweet Basement

It's been another crummy day.

Crummy because Kevin Richards shoved me into my locker again and was too smart to hang around and make himself late for gym. Crummy because Gianna wasn't at lunch. Crummy because I wanted to go home and try fixing the stupid toaster again, but instead, I'm here at the clinic after school for rabies shot number two.

"Kirby?" A nurse calls me in for my shot. She's bright and chirpy and irritating to death.

"Well, we're not in a very chipper mood today, are we?" she says, and clucks her tongue on her top teeth. "But I guess if we're getting poked in the arm, that's understandable." She wipes my arm with rubbing alcohol and gives me the shot. "There. You stay out of the bat cave now."

It's a double-crummy day when I get home.

Packing up all your stuff—everything you own in the world—and cramming it into seven cardboard boxes has a way of making you feel pretty insignificant.

The planetarium does that, too. When you're at a show and they zoom out from Earth to the solar system and then the whole universe and Earth is so small it's not even a speck anymore. But that makes you feel small in a good, awestruck sort of way.

Packing your stuff in old vodka boxes—some of them have ants crawling on them from sitting on the sidewalk outside Bell's Liquor—is completely different.

"Take your shoes off!" Aunt Becka stands at the top of the white-carpeted stairs that lead up to her gourmet kitchen and scowls down at my sneakers. My arms are full of books in a box, so I try stepping on one heel with the other foot. I lose my balance, spill half the books onto the slate floor, and fall against the wall.

"Careful of the art!"

I'm at least three feet away from the picture, a painting of a grumpy lady staring out a window. She looks about as happy to be here as I am.

I take off my shoes and start picking up books.

"Really, Laurie. You said he'd be no trouble."

Mom sets down a box of nursing books and wipes hair from her eyes with her sleeve. "He is no trouble, Beck. Kirby's a good kid."

Aunt Becka wheels around, goes to the kitchen, and starts opening cupboards. "Let's see," she says loud enough for us to hear. "I'll have to do extra grocery shopping to take care of feeding company for . . . what . . . ? Two nights? Three? Four?"

Mom presses her lips together like she's afraid of what will get out if she loosens them up.

Aunt Becka is Mom's older sister. She wasn't like this when she and Mom were growing up. Mom says they were super close until Aunt Becka left for college. In her junior year, she met Richard—he was Professor Kline to her back then—dropped out of school, married him, and moved into his house.

This house. With the white carpet and sourpuss paintings. But without much of Richard now. He gets lots of research fellowships and travels to South America and Africa, which is probably good because when he is around, he's not the nicest guy. I've seen Aunt Becka with bruises on her wrist that look an awful lot like someone's hand wrapped around it—hard. I heard Mom try to talk to her about it when she and Aunt Becka had to work together to clean out Grandpa's house after he died three years ago. That was a rough year for Mom—the same year Dad left—but she still really wanted to help. Aunt Becka told her to mind her own business because obviously she didn't know anything about marriage.

"Take that downstairs, okay?" Mom nudges me with her knee, and I realize I'm holding her up, blocking the hallway with my box. I kick open the door to the basement and make it down the stairs without spilling more books.

I make five more trips from the car.

Shoes on. Outside. Shoes off. Downstairs.

Shoes on. Shoes off. On. Off. On. Off. On. Off. All under Aunt Becka's dirt-hating eyes.

"Why aren't we in the guest rooms upstairs?" I set down the last box, drop my backpack in a corner, and plop down onto the sofa bed that's pulled out with a set of folded sheets on top of the bare mattress. There's an air mattress next to it on the floor.

"Because Richard's coming home from Argentina tomorrow, and they may be having other company later in the week. One of Richard's visiting professors. Up." Mom motions me off the bed so she can make it.

"But it's empty now. Don't you think it's weird they've got this huge house and we're in the basement?"

"Kirby, it's temporary, okay? This is what Becka gave us, and if you haven't noticed, I'm not exactly buried in better offers." She spreads the sheet over the mattress.

"Because you won't call Dad for help."

"That's right." She tucks in the corners of the sheet. She doesn't look at me.

I stomp over to the corner where I dropped my backpack and slide down the wall until I'm sitting on the floor. I take out the GPS unit and start scrolling through the cache coordinates on there. If I had my bike, I'd have time to go look for one tonight, but Mom said I had to leave it locked up by our old place until we find somewhere else to live.

Mom holds a pillowcase in one hand and looks around. There aren't any pillows. She sighs and starts putting sheets on the air mattress. She doesn't ask for help, and I don't offer.

I glance at my backpack, where science and social studies homework are waiting. There's math, too, but I didn't write it down, and I can't call Gianna or Ruby because I'd have to ask Mom to use her phone.

"I'm going to see if Becka needs help with dinner." Mom heads up the stairs.

"I'll be here in the dungeon." I pull out my social studies book and notebook. We have to read pages forty-five through fifty and answer questions one to five on page fifty-one. They're easy—just copy-what-it-said-in-the-text questions. My brain might actually be able to handle this.

We're studying the civil rights movement. I read five pages about school integration in the fifties and the Little Rock Nine— the nine black kids who enrolled in Little Rock Central High School and had to stand up to a whole bunch of white parents who didn't want them there. All they wanted was an education so they could make their lives better. I turn to a clean notebook page and look for a pencil to answer the questions.

There are two in the front pocket of my backpack, but one's

brand-new, unsharpened, and the other broke at the end of yesterday's math quiz.

My pencil sharpener's screwed to the wall next to my closet at home.

No. Not home.

It's screwed to the wall at Mrs. Delfino's son's rental property.

I pick at the wood around the broken lead with my finger, trying to get some of it out in the open so I can write.

Little bits of pencil wood fleck onto the white carpet. Finally, a charcoal gray stub sticks out the end.

Question Number 1. Why were the Little Rock Nine prevented from entering their high school even after the integration ruling?

It's an easy question. The answer's probably right back on page forty-five, but it's a pain balancing the textbook and my notebook on my lap, and I can't concentrate and I don't feel like flipping back to check the answer.

Because life's not fair, I start to write.

The pencil breaks again before I get to the *F*.

CHAPTER 21
Home Sweet Pickup Truck?

I spend the rest of the week avoiding Gianna so I don't have to tell her what happened. I can't. Not after our conversation at lunch.

Gianna wants to go to that dance with me. I don't want her thinking about me as somebody in trouble. Somebody whose family got thrown out of their apartment. People like that are the ones you donate used clothes to. The ones you help when you bring in cans of corn for a food drive or drop money in a Salvation Army kettle at Christmastime. They're not your friends. Not guys you'd want to dance with.

So I keep myself busy. I don't even stop at my locker after school on Friday. I leave out that side door by the ISS room.

Mom's still at the hospital doing her required volunteer hours when I get home. Aunt Becka meets me at the door.

"Take those shoes off, and for God's sake be quiet," she hisses. I set my backpack on the bench so I can get my shoes off, but she grabs it and holds it out, waiting for me to take it back.

"Richard's sleeping." Aunt Becka's eyes dart toward the stairs and back to me. "He got in this morning, and he's not happy you're here."

That makes two of us, I think. She hands me the backpack, picks up my sneakers as if they're a dead animal, and holds them out, too. "Downstairs, okay?" She looks up the stairs again and bites her lower lip. "Just take everything down and be quiet."

I'm leaning against the wall doing my math homework with a pencil I borrowed from our librarian, Mr. Smythe, when Mom gets home. She must have gotten the same treatment, because she comes downstairs holding her white nursing shoes in one hand, juggling her purse and a pile of her textbooks in the crook of her other arm.

She puts everything down, ruffles my hair, and opens her mouth—probably to ask how my day was—but before anything comes out, a door slams upstairs. Loud.

"I still can't believe you didn't talk with me first, Rebecca!"

Mom sucks in her breath but doesn't say anything.

Upstairs, it's quiet for a second.

Then, Richard's voice booms again. "What?!"

Aunt Becka says something too soft for me to hear.

"You're bloody right it's not going to be for long. I have important papers stored down there. I'm not paying a four-thousand-dollar-a-month mortgage so you can run a homeless shelter out of my office!"

Loud footsteps clunk across the floor over our heads—Richard apparently doesn't take off *his* shoes when he comes in the house. Then the basement door swings open. Mom steps in front of me as Richard bullies into the room.

"Excuse me, Laurie." He pushes past Mom toward a desk that Aunt Becka must have moved to the back corner of the room. "I need some papers from *my* office." When he gets to the desk, he explodes again. "Rebecca!"

Aunt Becka creeps down the stairs. She reminds me of how I used to go into the basement in our own house when I was little. I thought there were monsters down there.

Here, there really are.

"Where are my notes from the Peru trip? You've moved everything around so I can't. Find. A blessed. *Thing!*" On the last word, his arm slashes across the desk, and papers fly all over the room.

A manila folder lands at my feet. I bend to pick it up, and Richard lunges at me.

"Give me that and get out of my way!" He grabs the folder and shoves me aside. My shoulder slams into the wall. The rabies shot shoulder. The slammed-into-my-locker-by-Kevin-Richards shoulder.

Mom takes my elbow, steadies me, and pulls me back into Aunt Becka's laundry room. She closes the door, but we still hear him screaming at Aunt Becka.

Finally, his footsteps thump back up the stairs, back across the floor over our heads, and Mom opens the door.

Aunt Becka's sitting on the pull-out sofa with her hands over her face.

Mom's quiet at first. She sits down next to Aunt Becka, puts her arms around her, and strokes the back of her smooth blond hair.

Finally, she looks up at me and says one word.

"Pack."

"Are you warm enough?" Mom whispers over to the passenger seat of the pickup truck. I'm curled up in the sleeping bag I used to take on camping trips with Dad. He got it for me when I was nine. If I push my feet to the bottom and stretch out, it doesn't even reach to my chest.

"I'm fine," I whisper back. I close my eyes again, but the lights in the hospital parking lot are motion-activated, so every time a car or ambulance drives by on the side road, a streetlight blasts on, right in the window and through my eyelids.

"Try to sleep," Mom says. "You have school in five hours."

In the morning, I wake up with a cramp in my left leg and the truck door handle poking into the top of my head. Mom's shaking my shoulder. "It's seven o'clock, hon," she says. "You need to go to the before-school program for breakfast, and then you can use the gym shower after recreation time. Everyone will think you're just showering after exercise. Here, put this in your backpack." She hands me a miniature bottle of hotel shampoo.

I look at the label. "Montreal Imperial Plaza Hotel? When did you steal this shampoo?"

"It was in the bag Becka gave me when we left."

I put the shampoo in my bag and remember Aunt Becka's face when she rushed up to hand Mom the bag as we left. She didn't say anything out loud. But her eyes said, *I wish you could stay.*

Mom's said, *I wish you could leave.*

She couldn't. And Mom wasn't about to stay after what happened with Richard. So we've been residents of the hospital parking lot all weekend. We also spent a bunch of Saturday at the public library. I hung out in the science section, and Mom went through every apartment listing in the newspaper. But she didn't find anything we could get without a security deposit up front, and we don't have six hundred dollars.

"Are you ready?" Mom starts backing the truck out of our parking spot.

I'd laugh if my legs weren't so sore from being folded up in this seat all night. "Well, let's see . . . clothes . . . yep, slept in them. Backpack . . . used it as a pillow. Fancy hotel shampoo for the homeless kid? Check. I guess I'm ready for school."

She steps on the brakes so hard my head jerks forward. Hers whips around so she's facing me. "You are not homeless. I know we've had a rough couple nights, but I'm taking care of this. Today."

My heart jumps. "Are you calling Dad?"

"No, I am not. I'm going to social services to see about help."

"Why won't you talk to Dad? I know you guys—"

"Kirby." She presses her lips together and looks up at the dome light. "Your father is not part of our lives right now. And he isn't going to be any time in the near future. He'll talk to you about why when he's ready. Lord knows when that will be, but I'm not calling and neither are you."

I'm in an awful mood. I'm cold. I'm tired. And I ought to shut up. But the angry voice rises in my chest and spills out before I can think. "You're being so stupid! I can't believe you're doing this to me just because you don't want me to see him. You're putting us through all this because you're too stubborn to call him. If Dad were here, I'd be taking a shower in a house right now, and I'd have slept in a bed last night instead of the seat of this stupid rusty truck, and none of this ever would have happened!" I feel tears, hot on my cheeks, and wipe them away fast. "Why won't you call him?"

My heart pounds, waiting for her to yell back.

Instead, she turns around, puts the truck in park, and rubs her forehead with her hands, like she's trying to wipe away all my words.

Finally, she turns back toward me. I'm ready for her to shout, but the quiet voice she uses is even worse.

"You have no idea—no idea—how much I would give to wave a magic wand and fix this. You can't begin to know—and I hope you never find out—what it's like to have your child sleeping in your vehicle because you can't pay rent." Her eyes shine with tears. "I will take care of this. I will. Not your father. Me. And I'm going to deal with it today. I'll pick you up after school."

I nod. I don't yell anymore. I don't say anything until she drops me off at school, where the other free breakfast kids are waiting for the doors to open at 7:15.

"I'll pick you up at two forty-five for your next rabies shot." Mom blows me a kiss. "Have a good day."

Not likely. The first person in the breakfast line is Kevin Richards.

CHAPTER 22
French Toast Sticks and Secrets

"Move over, Zigonski." Richards plunks down his tray of French toast sticks and peels the foil lid off his imitation maple syrup. He drinks it right out of the little plastic box and uses the strips of French toast to mop up what's left.

I slide down the table a ways and pick up my fork.

Kevin eyes my backpack on the floor next to me. "Did you do the social studies?"

"Yeah."

"Got it here?"

I sigh. Guys like Kevin are always trying to bum homework from guys like me. Usually, I can just walk away. Down the hall. Into my next class. But at the before-school program, there is no "away." Thirty kids whose parents can't afford breakfast are crowded into two long cafeteria tables. Three teachers with plastic coffee mugs in their hands guard the doors until it's time to go to the gym for the activity period.

Richards reaches down for my backpack.

"Get your hands off that!"

He stops. "I just want to borrow it. Geez. What's your problem?"

What's my problem? Everything I own that's not boxed up and shoved into a damp corner of Aunt Becka's basement is in there. That's what. "I'll get it," I say.

He pulls his half-done homework out of his social studies book and paws around in his backpack. "You got a pencil?" he asks.

I pull out Mr. Smythe's pencil and hand it to him. "I need that back." He nods, squints at my paper, and starts writing on his.

"At least change a few words," I tell him.

"These sound good, though."

While Kevin copies my answers to questions three through five, the rest of the breakfast table fills in. I've been eligible for the before-school program for years—ever since Dad left— because Mom's income put us in the category for free French toast sticks and fake syrup. I've just never come until now. I never realized how many people show up here every morning.

I would have expected to see Kevin and some other kids who live in the trailer park near the river—Randy and Dylan, Josh and his twin sisters, Kim and Bethany. But there's also Michael

Martino, whose mom works at the adult day-care center where Nonna goes. I thought she was a nurse. Don't nurses make enough money? There's Jessica Hawkins, the only kid who ever beats my score on a math test. And there's Ruby in line, smiling and talking to the cafeteria lady. I look around for someplace to hide, but that's impossible here.

"Hey there!" Ruby walks up and sits across from Richards and me. She doesn't look even a little surprised.

"Hey," I say.

"Here." Richards slides my homework back to me on the table, and I put it away, relieved to have something to do. Ruby raises her eyebrows but doesn't say anything about me letting him copy.

Kevin punches me in the shoulder but not as hard as usual. I think it might even be a friendly kind of tough-guy punch, like they do sometimes. "I'll catch you down in the gym," he says, and waves for Dylan and Josh to wait for him.

"You guys pals now?" Ruby picks up one of her French toast sticks and dips it into the syrup.

"Uh, no. He wanted my homework and I didn't have an escape route, so . . ."

"Gotcha." Ruby pulls the paper off her straw.

"So . . . uh . . . how's the bird thing going?" I ask.

"Really good," she says. "We've been working on the posters. You should come over to Gee's house later. We're going to do some more."

"Sure. I mean . . . maybe."

I take another sip of my milk and take another bite of French toast. It's cold now.

"I didn't know you came here. I mean, for the before-school thing," I say.

"Just sometimes at the beginning of the month," Ruby says, matter-of-fact. "That's when Mom's first paycheck goes all for rent and car insurance. Most of the time, though, I'd rather eat at home and walk with you guys, so that's what I do."

I pick up my milk again, but it's empty. I pretend to drink from the straw anyway because I don't know what to say. I mean, obviously I had noticed that sometimes Ruby walked with Gianna and me to school and sometimes she didn't. I'd never noticed it was always the first part of the month.

"I guess I didn't know that," I say finally.

She smiles. "You wouldn't. It's not a big deal. It's how we solve a problem, Mom and me, and it works fine. I just don't talk about it."

"Listen, about that—I mean, with me. I don't really want people to know I'm coming to this now. I mean . . . people here obviously know, but—"

"Gianna?" Ruby says.

I nod.

She picks up her tray, and I follow her to the garbage cans to dump our napkins and syrup cartons.

"I don't see why it's a big deal, but I won't say anything."

She turns and looks at me. "Is everything okay? I mean, I know it's probably a tough money time, but you're okay, right?"

Part of me wants to tell her about Mrs. Delfino's son and his letters. About the liquor store boxes with the ants crawling over my stuff. About Aunt Becka and her white carpet and purple-green bruises. About the hospital parking lot. About Dad, and how Mom still won't call him for help.

But when I see the worry in her eyes and the way she twists her hair while she waits for me to answer, I can't do it. Ruby's like the nicest person I know. She'll make this her problem, and it's not. It's ours, and hopefully, Mom's going to solve it today.

I'm going to do what I can, too, I decide. I'm going to find Dad, whether Mom wants his help or not.

"Yeah, everything's okay," I tell Ruby. "Same situation, really, with the rent and the first of the month and stuff. I probably won't even be here tomorrow."

"Good." Ruby lets out the breath she was holding. I'm glad I lied to her. "Let's go play dodgeball."

"Does Richards play?"

She laughs. "Yeah, but I'm always on his team because I help tutor him in Spanish sometimes in study hall. Stick with me and you won't be on the other end of his dodgeball arm."

Good. Because today is going to be tough enough without getting my face bashed in by a red rubber playground ball, too.

CHAPTER 23
The Red Door

"Hey! Wait up!" Gianna's backpack thumps against her back as she bounds down the steps to catch me on the way out of school. "Where have you been?"

"Just busy."

Busy trying to concentrate on classes while I wonder where I'm going to sleep tonight. Busy apologizing to witchy Mrs. Seymour because I was unprepared for English after Richards walked off with my only pencil at breakfast. Busy hiding out at the homework table in the corner of the library, using another one of Mr. Smythe's pencils to finish the science I didn't do last night. Busy *not* running into Gianna, so I wouldn't have to pretend I was having a good day.

Ruby catches up with Gianna, and they start to turn left, the way we always walk home. I sit down on the step.

Gianna stops. She looks back at me and frowns. "You're not walking with us? Aren't you coming for hot chocolate?"

I shake my head. "My mom's picking me up. Rabies shot."

"Gotcha," Ruby says. "Here she is." She nods to the white-and-rust truck like I didn't hear it coming. Mom's needed a new muffler on that thing for a month.

"See ya." I wave, toss my backpack in the truck, and slam the door.

"Got much homework?" Mom asks as if it's a normal day.

I'm too tired to not play along. "Math and social."

"Not too bad." She turns out of the parking lot toward the doctor's office. We stop at the red light just as Gianna and Ruby are walking up to it. I turn the other way.

"How was the before-school program?" Mom asks.

"Fine."

"Was breakfast good?"

"It was okay."

"What did you have?"

"French toast sticks."

"Oh." She turns onto Bridge Street and we pass Rand Park, where I'd be stopping to skip stones if I were walking with Ruby and Gianna. The lake is perfectly calm today, like the face of a mirror. I could get ten skips, no problem. I know what I'd wish for if I believed in stuff like that.

But I don't. Especially not now.

At the doctor's office, Mrs. Richards is at her receptionist desk when we walk in. "Oh, Laurie," she says. "I'm glad you're here with Kirby today. I have some more paperwork for you, and we still need that insurance card."

"Oh." Mom's face falls. She rummages in her purse and finally pulls out her wallet. She flips through cards and photos—there's still one of Dad in there—and finally pulls out an insurance card. "Here, I think."

"Hmm . . ." Mrs. Richard takes the card and pokes at her keyboard. "You know this expired at the beginning of the summer?"

"Oh. I didn't realize . . ." Mom blinks fast. She's always been a terrible liar.

"We'll still administer the shot today—we have to, according to state health regulations—but we'll need to send you the bill, okay?"

"Sure." Mom nods, even though another bill isn't okay. Where are they even going to send it?

I get my shot, and my arm is throbbing when we get in the truck. I have to reach across with my left arm to pull the door shut because my right one's so sore.

"So," Mom says, pulling out of her parking spot. "Not too much homework?"

"Mom?"

"Umm-hmm?" She checks over her shoulder and pulls out onto the street.

"Where are we going?"

"I have to swing by the diner and check my schedule for the rest of the week."

"I mean tonight. Where are we going to stay? Did you find us a new place?"

"Well, yes." She pulls into a parking spot along the curb by Alan's, turns off the car, and turns to me. "Sort of. For now."

"What's that supposed to mean?"

"Social services is working on something long-term. For now, we're going to be staying at the Community Hospitality Center." She says it fast, maybe hoping that if the words zoom by quick enough I won't realize what she's talking about. But I do.

"The church homeless shelter? Mom, are you out of your mind? I'm not going there. I'd rather sleep in the truck again."

"That's not an option. It's going to be below freezing tonight. The good news is that you can keep your bike there. I picked it up earlier."

"Mom!" I can't believe she thinks the bike fixes this. "We're seriously going to sleep in a homeless shelter with a bunch of creepy strangers?"

I know that's mean to say, but I've seen them standing outside the Community Hospitality Center when I used to go by on my paper route. There's always one lady with a grocery cart full of plastic bags. I don't know what's in them. There are two guys who stand leaning against the wall, in clothes so dirty you can't even see what color they're meant to be anymore. This other guy, Brother Vinnie, people call him, is always talking to himself. If you say anything to him, he screams, "Mind yer own business, will ya?! This is between us!" Maybe there are other people around, too, but I only notice the loud, scary ones.

"Kirby, that's not fair. Plenty of people—"

"Plenty of people go there because they *have* to. We don't have to. We don't need to have this problem at all right now, but we do because you're too stubborn to call Dad and ask for help. This. Is. So. *Stupid.*"

I can't stand it anymore. I grab my backpack, practically burst out of the truck, and start walking home.

I get past the diner. Past the CornerMart, where Mr. Mulcahy waves as he's getting in his delivery van. I don't wave back. I'm halfway up the next block when I remember.

Home isn't up there anymore.

I stop at the curb and turn. Slowly.

Back down the block, I can see Mom standing by the driver's side of the truck. Not looking mad or sad or upset. Just standing there. Waiting for me to remember and come back.

So I do.

I get back in the truck and slam the door shut and put my head down on the dashboard. It's cool against my forehead. I close my eyes.

Mom gets in, too. I don't look up when we pull away from the diner. I don't look up when we drive down Washington Street, past Gianna's house. I don't look up when we turn at the corner at our old apartment. I don't even look up when the truck stops. The engine goes quiet. Mom's keys jangle as she drops them into her purse.

"Kirb." I feel her hand on my arm. "I know you don't under-stand why your father isn't involved in this. But trust me, get-ting in touch with him right now won't help. It won't. And I really need . . ." Her voice breaks, and her hand goes away.

I look up. She's blinking as fast as she can, but it doesn't stop the tears.

"I need you to be with me through this," she says quietly. "You're all I have."

For a minute, I'm angrier than I was before because she's making it so hard to be angry, and I *am* angry. I am.

But I need her, too.

I step out of the truck and look up at the steeple of Lakeland Unitarian Church. It looks taller than it did all the times I came by on my paper route. Like it's more of a big deal. I guess it is today.

Mom hands me a duffel bag from the truck bed, slings her bag with her nursing books over her shoulder, and lifts her suit-case. I lock my bike to the rack out front. We walk along the side of the building until we reach the red door of the small brick addition the church added on a few years ago with funds they raised to help the poor.

That's us now.

The poor.

I look over at Mom and catch her staring at the Community Hospitality Center sign on the door like she's thinking the same thing. This is a place for the poor. The unfortunate. The homeless.

I open the red door, and we walk through.

CHAPTER 24

What's the Scoop?

Spaghetti sauce.

The smell wraps me in a warm blanket as soon as I get inside. At first I think we've gone in the wrong door and crashed somebody's church supper.

But then I see the people sitting in the folding chairs, hunched over their plates on the tables. Shopping Cart Lady is there on the end with her cart parked next to her. I see a couple other guys I've seen in the line outside. There's Brother Vinnie, dipping his bread into the sauce.

And there are kids. Small kids. One little dude with blond hair and a spaghetti sauce face—he must be about five or six years old—keeps missing his mouth with the spaghetti and is wearing a lapful of it. His mom has a ponytail the color of sand and looks like she's barely out of high school. She licks her napkin and tries to wipe the sauce off his face while he squirms.

"Mrs. Zigonski?" A tall, thin guy with shaggy white hair and a white beard steps up to us. "Ted said you'd be here around dinnertime. I'm Rob Thomas, the site director. It's a pleasure to meet you." He reaches out to shake Mom's hand, as if he's doing business with her at a bank instead of checking us into a shelter.

"Thank you," Mom says. She looks surprised, too. "When I talked with Ted at the office earlier, he wasn't sure what kind of . . . uh . . . space you'd have available tonight." She looks around, probably wondering the same thing I am. The building's not big. Where are all these people going to sleep?

"Actually, your timing is good. One of our family rooms opened up this afternoon." Rob Thomas looks down at a clipboard in his hand and taps his pen on it. "We've been full for the past two weeks, since it started getting colder."

Brother Vinnie shuffles up to us in boots so old the toe isn't even attached to the sole anymore. He looks at Mom and me. "You better leave my stuff alone." He nods at the brown duffel bag slung over his shoulder. "Understand?" I nod.

"I'm sure you have nothing to worry about with these fine folks, Vinnie. You're in bunk fifteen tonight." Rob Thomas pats Brother Vinnie on the shoulder and guides him into the hallway toward a door that says "Men's dorm."

"Sorry," Rob says. "Vinnie and the other guys who are in and out stay in the dorm. It can get a little noisy there sometimes.

And a little rough, frankly, despite our best efforts. That's why we established family rooms a few years ago."

Mom nods. "Thanks. It will be nice to have some privacy."

"It's not private exactly." Rob Thomas checks his clipboard again. "The rooms are set up with four bunk beds, so you'll be with another woman and her son. We have a curtain down the middle for privacy. Hey, Heather!" He calls to the woman with the sand-colored hair. She leaves the little boy at the table, rolling his bread up into a tight little dough ball in his hands, and comes over.

"Heather, this is Laurie Zigonski and her son, Kirby."

"I go by Zig," I say.

She lifts her eyes from the floor for a second, says, "Hi" so I can barely hear it, and drops her head again.

My mom holds out her hand. "It's good to meet you, Heather. You have quite a fine young man over there."

Heather looks back at the table, where the boy is trying to stuff the whole bread ball into his mouth at once. When she turns back, she's smiling a little. "Thanks," she says, and shakes Mom's hand. Heather's is red and chapped.

Rob Thomas looks down at his clipboard again just as the door opens and two older teenagers come in. One has long black hair and an army jacket. The other one has short, spiky brown hair and a gray T-shirt and jeans. A worn-out guitar case is slung over his back. Rob glances at them, holds up a finger, and turns back to us. "So you'll be in room five tonight. Heather, you'll show them where the bathroom and showers are?" She nods and Rob jogs over to talk to the new guys.

"Thanks for offering to . . . uh . . . show us around," Mom says.

Heather nods again and looks like she wants to say something but doesn't know what. She sticks her hands in the front pockets of her jeans and pushes them in deep, like maybe that's where she left all her words.

Finally, she tells Mom, "This place is okay so far, in case you're worried about it. I was. They say they're gonna find us an apartment pretty soon. Me and Scoop here." She nods to the boy at the table. He's holding his napkin up to his face and has stuck his tongue through it.

"Scoop?" I say.

"His name's Anthony James," she says. "But we call him Scoop since he got old enough to talk. He's like a newspaper reporter, asking all kinds of questions."

"It's just the two of you, then?" Mom says.

"It is now. We left," Heather says. She blinks fast, like Mom does when she's trying not to cry. It doesn't work for Heather either. A tear slips out. When she pulls her hand from her pocket to wipe it away, I see bruises on her wrist like Aunt Becka's.

Mom sees, too. Her eyes cloud over, and she puts her hand on Heather's shoulder. "I'd like very much to visit with you and your son, but I'm thinking Kirby and I should wash up and have some food while it's hot. We'll see you in the room later on."

Heather nods. "Come on, Scoop." He jumps up and runs to her, crashing into her legs so hard he almost knocks her over. She's really skinny for a mom. "Let's go to the library and do some puzzles before bed."

"Will you read me *Library Lion*?" he asks, and I smile. Kids love that book. Gianna's little brother, Ian, never gets tired of it either. It's about this lion who walks into the library and decides to stay. So he helps out dusting and shelving books and listens to the stories, but he doesn't follow the rules exactly, so they throw him out into the rain. But then at the end, they realize what a good guy he was and let him come back, and he's all warm and cozy there again. I can see why Scoop would like it.

"I'll read it," Heather says. "*Once.* Not six times like last night." She takes his hand, and they head to a side room with beanbag chairs and a little bookshelf while Mom and I catch the end of the food line.

The spaghetti sauce is the best thing that's happened to me all week. You'd think it would be crummy sauce out of a jar, but this tastes like the stuff Nonna makes, and she was born in Italy. Mom says it's because church ladies volunteer to make dinner here three nights a week.

By the time we clear our paper plates, use the bathroom, change into sweatpants and T-shirts, and find room five, I'm wiped out. Heather and Scoop are already in one set of bunk beds. Heather's in the top bunk flipping through a *People* magazine. Scoop's in the bottom bunk—not happy about it.

"I want to sleep up there," he says, kicking the mattress above him.

"Quit it. I said no. It's too high."

"It's boring down here," he says. "Hmph." Then he spots Mom and me. "Oh, hi. My name is Scoop, remember? But not really. Really, it's Anthony James, but I like Scoop so call me that, okay?" I nod. "And I know you're Mrs. Zigonski, and you're her son Kirby who really wants to be called Zig instead, and I'm supposed to be quiet and not bother you because it's your first night here and you're probably tired. Are you?"

The corners of Mom's mouth turn up. It's the biggest smile I've seen from her all day. "Well, yes, we're pretty tired, Scoop. Not too tired to make a new friend, though."

That was a big mistake. Not only is Scoop our new friend; he's our new best friend forever.

I toss my backpack into the top bunk and start to climb up after it.

"Hey, Mom, see that?" Scoop says. "Zig's sleeping in the top bunk."

"He's a bit older than you," my mom says, trying to help out.

"How old is he?"

"Thirteen."

Scoop looks at me like he's trying to decide if Mom's telling the truth. Finally, he nods. "My cousin is thirteen. She lives in Ohio and has a smart mouth and is going to be the death of Aunt Molly and Uncle Joe."

"Anthony James!" Heather sits up and leans down to glare at him.

"That's what Aunt Molly says." He turns back to me. "Do you have a girlfriend?"

"No," I say. But Gianna pops into my head. Does that mean maybe I do? There's the whole dance conversation, and we always walk to school together. I knock twice on her door on my way by, and we sit on the porch and wait for Ruby, and we always walk together. Always until this week. What am I going to tell her tomorrow when I'm not there again?

"I don't believe you," Scoop says.

"What?"

"I don't believe you. I think you have a girlfriend. What's her name?"

"Anthony James! Will you leave these people alone?"

Mom reaches over to pull the curtain across the room.

"Okay, okay . . ." Scoop settles back onto his pillow but tilts his head out again and whispers, "But I still don't believe you."

CHAPTER 25
Believing in Magic

It takes me a few days, but by the end of the week, I have things at the shelter figured out and things feel almost normal. Okay, that's a lie. But they look normal anyway.

At first, I thought I'd ride my bike to school. But I figured out that if I leave the shelter at 7:30 and walk the long way to Gee's house, I go past our old apartment, so I'm coming from the same direction as always. Gee's always late, so she's never outside when I get there to see where I'm coming from anyway. And I don't have to go to the breakfast program anymore because there are showers at the shelter and they have toast and fruit cups in the morning. So that's a plus.

Friday morning, Gianna's extra late because she's lost her running shoes. She finally finds them in the laundry room, and it's a good thing, because by the time we leave her house, we have to run to make it to school before the homeroom bell.

"See you at lunch," Gianna says, and rushes down the hall to her locker.

I spend half the morning trying to figure out how to avoid lunch, but I'm finished with lunch detention, so I can't use that as an excuse not to show up anymore.

It turns out okay, though. I make sure I get there really late so Gianna's already through the line when the lunch lady punches in my number and the red bar that says "Free Lunch" pops up on her screen. They might as well slap a POOR KID sticker on your forehead before you sit down to eat.

I was eligible for free lunch before, but Mom never filled out the paperwork. She always made my lunch at home—a turkey and cheese sandwich or leftovers from dinner. It was better than the leathery, pink hockey puck sitting on my tray now, pretending it's ham. Try making a bag lunch in family room number five, though. Even if we had brought our food with us—which we didn't—so many things aren't around. Stuff I used to take for granted.

Plastic sandwich bags.

A snack when you feel like one.

Aluminum foil. I needed some the other night because Scoop's little battery-operated tow truck wouldn't tow anything, even with fresh batteries. It's a cheap toy, and stuff like that always breaks because the wiring isn't secure enough. I could see the problem but couldn't fix it. I had to wait for dinnertime so I could steal a little corner of the foil covering the rolls.

"Hey!" Gianna smiles a huge smile when I sit down. It makes me feel stupid for hiding out in the library last week. And besides, I really want her help looking for Dad.

"Want to go geocaching tomorrow?" I ask.

She raises her eyebrows and wiggles them at me. "Let me guess . . . You decided the bat-infested cave wasn't enough of a challenge, and so now you want to try to find one that's guarded by mutant rogue spiders."

"Like Aragog in *Harry Potter*?"

She grins and curls her two index fingers into fangs at the corners of her mouth, trying to look like a giant spider. She looks more like an Irish setter with buckteeth.

"Are you trying to look scary?" I say.

"My children need fooooood . . . ," she says in a scratchy voice, wiggling her finger-fangs.

"I'm serious," I say.

"I know." She lifts the top piece of whole wheat bread from her tuna sandwich and shakes off the lettuce and alfalfa sprouts her mom puts on there. "You're always serious. That's why Nonna says you're good for me." She glances up quick but then goes back to shaking sprouts.

"I . . . uh . . . yeah," I say. Nonna's always laughed about us getting together, but this is the first time Gianna's ever mentioned it. "So you wanna go geocaching?"

"I need to help Ruby with posters, but after that, I'll go. *If* it's just for fun." A Tater Tot flies across three cafeteria tables and lands in front of her. She picks it up and studies it. "Don't you think this is kind of shaped like Montana?" I look at it. It sort of is. Over by the window, where the Tater Tot came from, Kevin Richards is laughing with Ryan Larson as if no one's ever thought to throw a Tater Tot before.

"Geocaching's always for fun, isn't it? Except for the whole bat thing," I say.

"Yeah," Gianna says, "but you were getting kind of scary-intense about it. Like the whole world depends on you finding the geocache."

"It's not about finding the geocache . . . It's about—"

"I know it's about your dad. But, Zig, I still don't get why you think Senior Searcher is him. Even if it is, what makes you think you'll be able to find him? Your mom said he'd talk to you later, when he's ready. It's probably about the new girlfriend or something, but you need to relax. Why can't you just wait and see what happens?"

"You wouldn't understand." I pick up my tray and sling my backpack over my shoulder.

"You're making such a big a deal of this."

I stare at her. Such a big deal. That's easy to say when your family's all together and perfect and your father has his own business and pays the bills.

"See ya." I don't wave. I don't turn around. I go straight to the library, borrow a pencil from Mr. Smythe, and take out tomorrow's math homework.

But I'm so mad the numbers blur. The pencil breaks. I stare at fuzzy equations until the bell rings for science.

After school, I stall at my locker hoping Ruby and Gianna will walk home without me. They wait for me like always, so I have to pretend everything's fine. We stop at the park so Ruby can skip her rocks and make her stupid wishes and talk about her big plans for the city council meeting every time a heron flies over. We stop at the diner for hot chocolate—somehow there's still money for that, or else Alan isn't charging Mom for it. At about five, I wave goodbye to Gianna and Ruby when they go home to have dinner. Then I hang out doing homework at the counter until Mom's diner shift is over.

Mom and I get home—shelter-home—at around seven, which is a good time because dinner's ready, but it's not too early. The shelter has a rule that you have to be gone during the day—in school or out looking for a job or an apartment or doing something to prove to somebody that you don't plan to stay forever. If you need someplace to go during the daytime, you go to the social services office downtown. Adults can use their phones, and little kids can play in the toy space. That's where Scoop was this afternoon while his mom made calls on part-time jobs.

"Hey, Zig! Zig! Know what I learned today?" He comes running up with orange-yellow sauce around his mouth. Macaroni and cheese night.

"What?"

"A magic trick. You wanna see?"

"Sure."

"Okay . . ." He holds out his hand, faceup, and puts a quarter in his palm. "I, the great and powerful Scoop, will now make this quarter *disappear!*" He waves a white handkerchief over his hand a few times and then lets it rest there. Then he picks it up again and hands it to me. I can feel a coin inside the cloth. "Okay . . . now you have the coin, right?"

"Right."

"Okay. Now I'll say the magic words." He opens his mouth but nothing comes out. "Hold on . . . I forgot them."

"Usually, any old magic words will work," I tell him. "As long as the magician is great and powerful."

"Right," he says, and starts waving his hand in fast circles around my hand that's holding the handkerchief. "Hickedy-Wickedy-Pickety-Slickety-Boo-Too-POO!" On the "POO" part, he grabs the handkerchief, whips it out of my hand, and shakes it. "See? The coin is gone!"

I nod. "Pretty impressive. Can I see that handkerchief again?"

He stares down at it in his hand. "No."

I grin. "How come?"

"Because I'm the great and powerful Scoop and I say so."

"Oh."

"Also because the coin you had in your hand just now is really a secret coin I had hidden in this cool pocket the whole time."

He pulls back a piece of cloth that's Velcroed to the corner of the handkerchief to reveal a quarter. Then he reaches into his pocket and pulls out another one. "Here's your real quarter."

"You really had me for a minute there."

He nods. "I know. When Rob showed me, I thought he could really make coins disappear. And then he said he could make them appear again, too, and I was thinking how cool because then you could make lots and lots of them appear and you'd have enough money to pay for a house with a tree fort and your mom wouldn't have to find a job. You could live there and play in your tree fort all day."

I smile. "That would be pretty cool."

"But then he showed me the stupid secret pocket and ruined everything."

"Sometimes it's better not to find things out."

He nods. "Did you ever find something out and then wish you didn't know?"

"Hardly," I say, thinking about everything I can't find out. Where Dad is. Why he hasn't called. Why Mom's so mad at him she won't let me see him. Why she's mad enough to have us living here, in a place where little kids can't even believe in magic for more than a few minutes.

CHAPTER 26
To Skip or Not to Skip

"What are you going to do all day?" Mom ties on her apron for a double shift at the diner. "I'm worried about you being out on your own."

"I'm going to geocache," I tell her. "So I can get some exercise and fresh air." Moms never argue with exercise and fresh air. The only thing better would be if I told her I'd eat broccoli on the way.

"Do you want a ride somewhere?"

I shake my head. "I'm going to ride my bike."

"Okay, but be careful. And be back by seven. I'll be here by then."

Even though I have a stop to make first, I turn on the GPS as soon as I get outside. I love fiddling with the coordinates. I've entered home—what used to be home, anyway, and now the shelter, school, the diner, and most of Dad's geocaches. I unlock my bike, hop on, and head for the library. I want to get on a computer so I can check the coordinates on the last one. I was entering it in a hurry because Mom was hovering.

Except in the mornings when I'm trying to look like I'm coming from there, I don't like to pass by our old apartment. I'm still afraid I'll forget it's not our place anymore, take the porch stairs two at a time, and barge in on whoever lives there now. I don't know who moved in. Somebody who has enough money to pay Mrs. Delfino's son his rent on the first of every month, I guess.

I look up the block to see if there's a new car parked outside. It's hard to tell with street parking because if it's busy, people park any old place. There's a blue pickup truck that I don't recognize, though. And a yellow Nissan Sentra. And something that looks like it might be an old convertible. They could definitely afford to pay rent on time.

And then I see something awful. Gianna and Ruby. Practically running up the street toward the old apartment. Ruby stops to smell the flowers Mrs. Delfino planted by the porch, while Gianna hops up the steps and knocks on the door. She turns my way, and I ride my bike off the sidewalk and duck behind a hedge.

Through the prickly branches, I see Gianna knock again, harder. She peers in through the storm door. Can she see that all our stuff is gone? Is somebody else's stuff in the kitchen?

She looks around and finally goes down the stairs, where

Ruby's waiting. They walk back toward Gianna's house, and I breathe out a big whoosh of a relief. No one new has moved in. No one is living in our apartment.

And Gianna hasn't found out.

When I get to the library, it's busy enough that nobody asks if I need help when I sit down at one of the public computers and log onto the geocaching website. I enter "Senior Searcher" in the search box and wait.

I hope there's a new entry. A new cache Dad planted or one that he found—something to show me he's still in town.

Finally, the page loads, but there's nothing new. Dad's not geocaching these days. What's keeping him so busy? Too busy for his hobby. Too busy to call. Too busy to bother caring about me.

I check the coordinates for the last cache I wrote down, and it's a good thing, because I had the latitude right, but the longitude was totally wrong. I look around for a pencil to write it down, but the only one on the desk is broken.

"Here." A smiley-face pencil with a bright yellow background appears in front of my nose. I turn around, and there's Gianna. She holds the pencil up to her face and smiles a big cheesy grin.

"See the resemblance?" She holds the pencil out to me again. I take it. "I'm sorry," she says. "I know this is important to you, and I shouldn't have given you such a hard time about it. So I'm here to help." She turns so I can see her backpack, green with purple flowers and bulging at the seams. "I have water, trail mix, a bunch of little plastic animals that Ian doesn't play with anymore—those are to leave in the caches in case we want to take something—rain ponchos, a topographical map of Lakeland and the surrounding townships, and a first-aid kit. In case you find any more hostile geocache guards like the bats."

"They weren't hostile, really. I didn't get bit. I just have to have the shots because one touched me."

"Come on," Gianna says. "Ruby's waiting at the park. It's a good skipping day."

I use the smiley pencil to write down the coordinates for Dad's last cache, stand up, and tuck the GPS unit into my backpack. It's hard to stay mad at someone who passes out smiley-face pencils.

"It's not much of a skipping day," I say. Wisps of smoke-gray clouds are moving fast across the sky as we head for the park. I walk my bike so I don't get ahead of them. "Too windy."

Gianna turns so her massive backpack almost bumps me off the sidewalk. "You have a crummy attitude. You ought to skip stones like the rest of the world and see what happens. Not everything has to be perfect. Sometimes, rocks skip fine when the waves are big and the wind is blowy. They skip anyway. Even if *you* think they shouldn't."

Ruby waves to us, and we walk across the grass, past a couple toddlers fighting over a dump truck in the sandbox, to meet her.

I park my bike, and Ruby hands me a stone. "I challenge you

to a skip-off, Kirby Zigonski." She curls her arm into her body and flings hers like a Frisbee. It skips once, gets caught on a wave, and takes a hard right turn. I think it's going to plunk and disappear, but it takes seven or eight more tiny little skips before it sinks.

There's applause behind us. It's Mr. Webster. "That's some skipping arm you have."

"She practices a lot," Gianna says. "We're here almost every day after school."

"My wife used to enjoy this park so much when she could get out more," he says, looking into the waves. "She loves watching the birds."

"Me too." Ruby skips another stone—nine this time—and Mr. Webster claps.

She curtsies, waves to an imaginary crowd, and points to me. "Your turn."

I look down at the stone she gave me. It actually has great properties for skipping. It's the size of one of the school cafeteria chocolate chip cookies—just big enough to cover my palm. It's perfectly flat and round, without even the tiniest bump or crack to mess things up. But then the wind gusts, and the waves kick up.

"It's not going to work. I forfeit." I drop the stone at my feet. Nothing's going to work until I find my dad and he can come fix this mess. And I want to get on with it. "Can we go now?"

Gianna nods. But she bends down and picks up the stone I dropped. I turn to leave the park, but she tugs on my backpack. I stop.

"You should keep this one," she says. "It's perfect. Keep it for a better skipping day." She unzips my backpack and drops the rock inside. It clunks against the GPS unit. "Now let's go look for your dad."

CHAPTER 27
Marble and Mysteries

The GPS unit points us toward Flying Bridge Marina, over the river off Bridge Street. As soon as we cross the bridge, the arrow tells us to go another 128 yards to the south, but Ruby heads right for the docks instead.

"I want to see if there are still boats in." The wind that comes from the south all summer long has changed seasons; it's blowing out of the north, kicking up big waves.

"Just one sailboat," Gianna says as we turn the corner of the marina building. She points to the lone mast silhouetted against the clouds, tipping back and forth in the swells.

"Oh, look!" Ruby points to the end of the last dock. A great blue heron stands on the last weathered plank, like it's getting ready to do a trick off a swimming pool diving board. It turns to look at us, and its long beak points out toward the islands.

"He looks worried," Ruby says. "I bet he knows the Smugglers Island meeting is happening soon."

"Right." I snort out a laugh. "Maybe he's been making posters."

Ruby whips around and looks so mad I take a step back. Ruby never gets mad. "Just because something isn't important to you doesn't mean it's not important," she says.

"I . . . sorry." I watch the heron bend its long legs, lift its wings, and pump them to lift its body from the gray boards. It flies off, toes pointed behind it. When I turn back to Ruby, she's gone—past the last dock on the rocky beach, skipping stones.

"I know you've been busy," Gianna says, and tugs my sleeve to start walking toward Ruby. "But you should know she's been spending pretty much her whole life working on posters and getting people signed up to speak at that meeting. It's important to her, even if it seems weird to you. You ought to understand about that sort of thing." She nods at the GPS unit in my hand, pointing past Ruby's stone-skipping spot down the lake.

I nod, just as we reach Ruby. "It is important," I say. She looks up. "I'll be there, Ruby. At the meeting."

"You will?"

"Yep—promise."

"Thanks." She smiles and backhands one last stone. It skips about twelve times.

"How do you always do that?"

"I expect it to skip," she says, lifting her backpack from the pebbles. "Sometimes believing's enough."

"Well, you can believe all you want, but unless we walk another ninety-six yards that way, we're never going to find this thing." I lock my bike to a post and start following the arrow.

"Aren't the railroad tracks up here?" Gianna asks as we start off again. "That's a weird place for a geocache."

We're walking right along the tracks now. There's no train noise, but Ruby keeps checking behind her. "This can't be right," she says. "Are you sure you entered the numbers right?"

"Yeah, I checked twice."

"What's the cache called?"

"Train Wreck."

"That's encouraging. Did this one have a clue on the website?"

"Yeah. I brought it, but you're only supposed to use that if you're stuck." I look down at the GPS unit. It says we're within three yards of the cache. I look around. Aside from the railroad tracks we're walking on, there are a bunch of prickly bushes on our right and about a five-foot drop-off to the lake on our left.

Gianna peers into the bushes but gets thorns stuck in her hair. "Ow!"

Ruby helps her untangle. "I'd say this qualifies as stuck. Get figuring, code-master."

I pull out the notebook paper from my back pocket. I wrote the code down in pencil. It's already faded to a tired light gray, but I can still read it.

ZKDW PLJKW KDYH EHHQ D PRQXPHQW
ODQGHG LQ WKH ODNH.

ABCDEFGHIJKLMNOPQRSTUVWXYZ
DEFGHIJKLMNOPQRSTUVWXYZABC

I set to work with Gianna's smiley-face pencil while she and Ruby poke around the bushes.

"It's probably not even legal to have a geocache here," Ruby says, looking up and down the tracks.

"Hold on." I'm halfway through the code. "In a minute we'll know if we're on the right track or not, but I'm sure I—"

"Ow!" Gianna's hair is stuck again.

"Here." Ruby starts untangling.

"Okay, I've got the clue," Gianna says. "We're definitely in the right place. It says—"

"Shhh . . . ," Ruby says. She stops untangling. "Listen."

I stop to listen. It's the rumble of a train. Getting louder. And closer.

"Ow!" Gianna tries tugging her hair out of the thorns, but it gets more tangled.

"Hold on," Ruby says. "There!" All three of us stare up the tracks at the front of a train. It's coming slowly. But it's coming.

"Thorn bushes or lake?" Ruby says, peering over the drop-off.

"Lake," Gianna says, eyeing the thorn bushes that tried to eat her hair. "We can climb down—look." She sits on the edge of the bank, then flops over onto her stomach and finds a foothold in the rocks. She looks over her shoulder. "Come on . . . the water's barely up to these top rocks, even with the waves. We can wait down here."

The train's slowed down—we probably would have had time to backtrack and get out of the way, but now Ruby and I are halfway down, too. I find a good handhold in the rocks and stretch my right foot down toward the flat rocks below. I'm almost there, so I let go and jump down. My foot lands on a slick of slimy green algae and flies out from under me. I go down hard on my knees as a big wave splashes all the way up to the rock wall.

At least I kept the clue dry.

"What's it say?" Ruby asks as I wipe lake slime off my knees.

"It says—"

"Hold on!" Gianna shouts. "Train!"

The train—made up of eight rusty freight cars—rumbles past above us. The rocks tremble like there's an earthquake. The whistle blasts. Then the train clicks and chugs its way south to some other old railroad town.

"Okay." Gianna leans in close to me.

"It says, 'What might have been a monument landed in the lake.'"

"In the lake?" Gianna says, and together, we turn and stare into the waves. "Hey!" Gianna bends over, unlaces her red high-tops, and pulls them off, along with her purple socks.

"Careful!" Ruby says as Gee slides out onto the slimy stuff.

The cold water turns her skin bright red. Her toenails are painted green, so her foot looks all Christmasy. "Grab my hand, okay?" Gianna reaches out, and I take it. She leans way over into the water. "Got it!" She stands up clutching a perfectly flat rectangle of white rock about the size of a cell phone and hands it to me.

"It's marble," I say, running my hand over its cold smooth surface. I look out and see bigger slabs in the water. "What might have been a monument landed in the lake . . . I bet a train dumped a load of marble here!"

I turn and start to climb up the rock face again, but Ruby tugs my sweatshirt. "Look." She points to a corner of pink plastic sticking out from one of the crevices.

I pull it free, brush away a couple dried-up spiders, and pry off the lid. "It's more rocks." I pick up another chunk of marble and see a folded paper underneath. "There's a note in this one!" I slide out the single piece of unlined white paper, unfold it, and read.

Congratulations! You have found the Train Wreck cache. You've also found the site of a great Lakeland disaster. In the spring of 1897, there was a tremendous rain that made the ground soft. When a train carrying marble from the quarry in Eastville rumbled through, the earth under the tracks gave way, and the train derailed, spilling its cargo into the lake. The largest pieces still rest on the bottom, while many medium-sized slabs have been taken for garden stones. The smallest remain—reminders that nature will always get the best of us.

To log your find, please remove one piece of marble from the container. Take it home with you or plant it in another geocache along the way to see where it ends up. Then find another piece of about the same size. Write your name and the date on it, and leave it in the cache for the next brave soul who finds Train Wreck.

"Here." Gianna hands me the piece she pulled out of the lake and fishes around in her backpack again until she finds a permanent marker. "Sign it, Zig. You can be our spokesman."

I start to make a *Z* but catch myself. Instead, I write "Circuit Boy was here."

When I tuck the geocache container back into its spot, something else sticking out from the rocks catches my attention.

"Hey!" I pull out a little hardcover book with a plain green cover. The pages are damp, but I flip through them. "This is somebody's journal," I whisper. Pages and pages of dates and entries, with sketches of plants and trees and stuff.

"Wow." Gianna leans over me to look at a sketch.

"And look," Ruby says, reaching out to stop me on a page with numbers on top. "That's a geocache coordinate, isn't it? I bet this is somebody's geocaching journal."

"And she just left it here?" Gianna takes the journal from me and flips through again. "No one would do that on purpose. These sketches are gorgeous." Gianna stops on a page with a sketch of a great blue heron flying between clouds. "I bet whoever left this put it down to put the cache back in the wall and forgot it," she says.

"Is there a name in it?" Ruby asks. Gianna flips back to the front of the book, to the page right inside the cover, and stares.

"Well?" Ruby says. But Gianna doesn't hand the journal to Ruby. She hands it to me. Still open to the page inside the cover. I look down and read the inscription:

Geocaching Journeys:
Senior Searcher

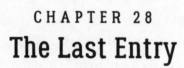

CHAPTER 28
The Last Entry

I've only been in bed five minutes when Scoop kicks the bottom of my bunk. "Hey, Zig?"

"Yeah?"

"Wanna play Uno?"

"Not now—you're supposed to be asleep." His mom asked me to keep an eye on him while she's talking with a job counselor in the common area. Our family room light is off, but I have a few Christmas tree bulbs rigged up to a nine-volt battery and clipped to my bed rail so I can read. I lean over the edge of my bunk until I can see Scoop.

"Will you read to me?" he asks.

"We read *Library Lion* three times, Scoop. Go to sleep." I flop back in my own bed and open Dad's journal. I've been reading it over and over, all weekend. I can't help thinking he left it on purpose, for me to find. But I must be missing something—the part that says how to find him.

I flip another page, and Scoop starts kicking at the top bunk. *Thump. Thump. Thump.*

"Quit it." I check my watch. 9:30. Half an hour until his mom gets back.

"What are you reading up there?" he asks.

"Something my dad wrote a long time ago."

"Oh." *Thump. Thump. Thump.* "Know how come I like *Library Lion*?"

I give up. I close the journal and lean down. "How come?"

"Because the lion gets to stay. And because the mean guy turns into a good guy."

"Yeah, well . . . don't count on that happening too often in real life."

He's quiet for a minute before he starts kicking again. *Thump. Thump.*

I go back to Dad's journal. There are pages and pages here, but almost none of it is personal. It's all about how inspirational the trees and the rocks are. I never knew Dad was so into nature. He always seemed more interested in his cell phone than the trees when we went camping.

But there's one part I read yesterday that I want to find again. One part that brings him out of the woods and away from the birds and the rocks. Back to Dad voice. Here it is. Dated

June 21 of this year. The second from the last entry, almost covered up by a sketch of a huge fern.

> I came out for quiet, but the woods scream "New! New! New!" in their noisiest greens this afternoon. Spring comes late to the mountains, but when it comes, it explodes with life and color. Too much for my eyes today. It's been a day of goodbyes, and goodbyes should always be in black-and-white, like kisses in old movies.
>
> Tried talking with L one last time before I left. She wouldn't even look at me. I will always wonder if she understood why I made the choice I did. I so wish I could turn back the calendar to our happy years together.
>
> The mosquitoes are out. Time to head home.

"Hey, Zig?" It's Scoop, quieter.

"Yeah?"

"Is that book that your dad wrote a good book?"

I flip through pages and pages of coordinates and notes on the weather and the color of the pitcher plant flowers and salamanders. Almost nothing that means anything to me. "Not really," I say. "Parts of it are okay, I guess."

"Is your dad nice?"

I let that one hang between the bunks for a minute before I answer. "He's great when he's around. But he's not around much."

"Oh." *Thump. Thump.* "My dad's nice sometimes, too. But

then he yells and stuff. I'm not allowed to see him anymore. I wish I could, though. Know what I mean?"

I leave Dad's journal on the bunk and climb down the ladder. "Move over." Scoop sits up cross-legged and slides over to make room for me. "Sometimes," I tell him, "you can love somebody and miss them and still have it not be a good idea for you to be with them. At least not right now."

"But people can get different, can't they? Like Mr. McBee in the book? He changes his mind and is a lot nicer to the lion."

I start to say Mr. McBee's not real. But something stops me. "Yeah, sometimes. But not always."

"Hey, Zig? How come your dad isn't here either? Is he mean sometimes, too?"

"No," I say. "He's never really mean. He's . . . super busy, I guess."

Scoop nods. "Will you read me some of that book he wrote?"

I shake my head. "No, but if you promise to go to sleep right after, I'll read *Library Lion* one more time. I'll go get it from the library."

I start to get up, but he grabs my pajama sleeve and pulls me back. "Here." He pulls it out from under his pillow. He must have brought it back after dinner.

He hands me the book. "You can start right there."

It's already open to the page where Mr. McBee goes to find the lion in the rain and invites him to come back to the library. Back home.

CHAPTER 29
Things to Avoid

"Have a good day," Mom says as I head out the shelter door to face another one.

Day fifteen.

I wonder if she's counting.

Fifteen days since we walked through that door for the first time.

Fifteen dinners with Brother Vinnie and his imaginary friends.

Fifteen days of being a homeless kid, and here's the weird thing. I'm getting better at it.

Our first couple days at the shelter felt like they went on forever—the nights especially, with the coughing and arguing from the men's room, Scoop talking in his sleep. But you get used to those night noises, like you get used to owls and crickets if you live in the country. Brother Vinnie is just louder and curses sometimes. You don't get that so much with crickets.

But I've mostly fallen into the routine of not having a regular place to live.

Morning shower.

School.

Library.

Homework at the diner until Mom's done.

Late dinner.

Bed.

Then start over.

Unless it's a weekend. Then I go out geocaching. Sometimes with Gee and Ruby but not lately. Lately, I've been taking my bike and going alone. It feels more personal now, with the journal. Like this is something between Dad and me. Something I need to do myself.

In the past two weeks, I've found three more caches that the website says Dad found, too. One was wedged between two foundation rocks at the ice cream place on the water. "Sweet Rewards," it was called, and there were coupons for ice cream inside. No Dad clues, but I took a coupon and had a chocolate-chip-cookie-dough cone.

There was one hidden in some bushes in the trailer park. The nearby river floods sometimes, so the people in the trailers have to go to the shelter for a few days almost every April. I think when that happened the cache got all wet, because the log book and trinkets were moldy, except for a little green plastic army guy, and he was missing his head. There was nothing from Dad.

Another cache was duct-taped under a board on the footbridge near school. I had to lean over the railing and balance on one foot to reach it. The cache was a film canister full of state quarters. I took Florida and left a Connecticut quarter I had in my pocket.

Shower. School. Library. Diner. Dinner. Bed. Geocache sometimes.

That's my things-to-do list now. It's short.

My things-to-avoid list is longer.

Mostly, that list is filled with people.

Brother Vinnie, because he still freaks me out by shouting at no one.

Kevin Richards, even though I haven't had to play him in dodgeball lately.

Gianna, because that November dance that she talked about is getting closer. I can't go to a dance wearing jeans and one of my four T-shirts that aren't locked in Aunt Becka's basement. And I can't tell Gianna why, so I don't tell her much of anything anymore. Not even hi some days.

Homework's on my list of things to avoid because there's no real time to get it done. I'm at the library after school, but that's the only chance I have to use the computer and go to the geocaching site. The diner's not quiet enough, plus sometimes I help bus dishes if they're busy. And the shelter's not really a place where you can get homework done. The guys in the men's bunk are always arguing, and Scoop's always asking questions, or somebody's looking over your shoulder at your math problems, and it's just dumb. There's no pencil sharpener either.

I'm also avoiding my last two rabies shots. I didn't get bit, anyway. It's not like you get rabies from having bat poop in your hair, right? Mom reminded me to stop by the doctor's office and have the shot and tell them to bill her.

"And send it where?" I asked her. "Should they address it to room five, the upper bunk?"

"I don't really care where the bill goes."

I nodded, but I didn't say I'd go. And I didn't. I went straight to the library after school instead and then complained later that my arm hurt. Mom never asked about the shot or how it went or when they wanted to be paid, so I figure she really didn't feel like talking about it either, and I was doing us both a favor by skipping it.

My new routine—my lists of things to do and things to avoid—works out great until somebody messes with it.

Like today, when I dump my backpack in our room and come out for dinner.

"Hey, Zig! Zig! You know how long the longest fingernails in the whole world are?" Scoop wiggles his hands at me.

"Are they yours?"

"No!" He laughs. "Do these look like they're twenty-four feet long?"

"That can't be right," I say. "It'd mean your fingernails would stretch from here to the end of the dinner line."

Scoop looks way down at the end of the table where the church ladies are serving salad and frowns. "Maybe it was twenty-four inches. But it's still pretty cool, isn't it?"

I nod and steer him toward the goulash. His mom got a job at the diner with Mom, and Rob agreed that Scoop could be at the shelter without her as long as there's somebody to babysit. That's me. So tonight, Heather's working late, and it's another *Library Lion* marathon in the library after we have our green Jell-O for dessert. Finally, Scoop goes to bed, and I climb into my bunk.

And I go nuts.

"Were you in my stuff?" I whip around so fast the bunk ladder comes unhooked and falls over onto the other bed, just missing Scoop. "Were you in my stuff?!"

"No! I was with you at dinner and you read to me. I wasn't even in here!" A tiny part of my brain registers how scared he is to see me mad, but the rest of it can't stop to think. I grab the ladder, hook it back onto the bunk, and climb up to where my stuff has been dumped in a big heap.

Math homework. Science book. Science binder with half the pages falling out now. Jeans. Three T-shirts. Underwear. Socks. I throw them into a messy pile and keep looking for Dad's journal. Finally, I find it shoved under my pillow.

But my GPS unit is gone.

"Stay here." Scoop curls his knees up under his chin and nods the tiniest bit. I fly out of the room and down the hall toward the men's bunk. It's that freak Brother Vinnie. Running around and talking to himself and stealing people's stuff. I pound on the door. "Open up!"

Vinnie doesn't answer the door. It's a new guy—short and muscular and bald, with sores on one side of his face. "New boy for the bunk?" His smile makes me want to punch him, too, but instead I push past him into the center of the room. It's lined with four bunks on each side. "Where's Vinnie?"

"You got a problem?" The bald guy steps up to me and points to a bed piled high with dirty clothes and blankets. "Vinnie ain't here."

I take long steps across the room to the bed and start ransacking the pile, throwing clothes on the floor. They smell awful, and I want to gag, but all I can think about is finding that GPS unit. What kind of a freak goes into a kid's room in a homeless shelter and steals the only thing he has that might help him? I *need* that GPS unit.

I'm shaking out the blankets when I hear boots on the wood floor behind me. "You wouldn't be looking for this, would you?"

The bald guy is standing there with my GPS unit in his hand.

"Give it to me!" I reach for it, but he steps back and holds up a hand to push me back by the shoulder.

"I might consider selling it to you if you're polite."

"You stole it!" I push forward, and the guy gives me a good

shove. I fly back against the bunk and land on Vinnie's dirty clothes.

I look up and glare at him. "It's mine. Give it back."

"What'll you pay for it?"

"If I had money, do you really think I'd be living in this dump? I need that. Just . . . give it to me. Please." That anger that clenched my throat slides down to a sick feeling in my stomach. Who do I think I am? And how stupid was it to come here? These guys are thieves and freaks. There's not a thing I can do to get my GPS back.

I look down. A big ant crawls toward my sneaker. I step down hard and hear its exoskeleton crunch.

"Hand it over," a low voice says. I look up and can't quite process what I'm seeing.

Another muscular figure—bigger than the bald guy. A fat, meaty hand held out. The bald guy puts my GPS unit in it, and the big hand reaches out to me. I ought to know that hand. It's shoved me up against lockers enough times. But for once, I'm thankful that Kevin is a beast who's three times the size of a normal eighth grader. That other guy wants nothing to do with him.

I take the GPS unit. "Uh . . ." What do you say when you run into your worst enemy at the homeless shelter, and he decides to save your butt from an even nastier bully? "Thanks. I . . . uh . . . thought Brother Vinnie stole it, so . . ."

Kevin shakes his head. "No way. Vinnie has a tough time,

and people get freaked out because he's always talking to himself, but he's okay. He'd never steal from a kid."

"Yeah." Now I'm the one who feels like a jerk. I look around. The bald guy has gone back to his card game as if nothing happened. Another guy's reading an old issue of *Sports Illustrated*. And Kevin's still standing in front of me.

"So. You're, like . . . here now?" he says.

"Kinda. Yeah."

"I figured somethin' was up with you."

"What do you mean?"

"You never have pencils I can swipe anymore."

"There's no sharpener here."

Kevin nods. "I know."

"So you've been here a while? How come I didn't see you?"

He shrugs. "Just got back. Place we tried to rent didn't work out."

"Oh." And they must not have had any family rooms left. So he's here.

"Well, that's a buncha garbage!" The bald guy slams down his cards and leaves the room.

"Yeah . . . well . . . I better go," I say. "I'm watching my mom's friend's kid."

He nods. "See ya."

"Yeah." I start to go but turn back. I feel like I should say something else. Kevin beats me to it.

"Listen . . . I'm not telling anybody," he says. "There's rules in here. You keep your mouth shut about who you see in the spaghetti line."

"Got it." On the way back to room five, I stop in the library to get *Library Lion*. Scoop's still on the bunk with his knees tucked under his chin. He doesn't look scared anymore. Just sad.

"Sorry," I say. "One of the mean guys took my GPS unit."

"I didn't do it," he says.

"I know," I say. "I'm sorry I got upset." I hold up the book. "Want me to read?"

He nods and stretches out his legs in his sleeping bag. "Start at the part where Mr. McBee turns nice."

"I know," I say. I had my finger in that page already.

CHAPTER 30
The Less Fortunate

On the morning of Halloween, Gianna whooshes into social studies as the bell rings, spilling colored pencils behind her. She drops a note on my desk.

"All right, that was the bell. Write down your homework," Mrs. Heath says. I slide Gee's note under my binder and take out my assignment book.

"For Monday, you'll read the New Deal chapter and do the questions. Then for Tuesday—"

She pauses and I look up from scribbling down the assignment. Kevin Richards just walked in without any of his stuff. Nothing sets Mrs. Heath off faster than a kid who shows up without a notebook and something to write with. Everybody knows. That's why everybody's stopped writing. They're waiting for her to erupt.

"Mr. Richards," she says. "How nice that you could make it."

Kevin doesn't say anything. He slides into his seat. He's in the front row, in the official troublemaker spot so she can keep an eye on him.

"Take out your assignment book, please," Mrs. Heath says, even though she can see he doesn't have it.

"I didn't bring it."

"Then take out a piece of paper on which to write down your assignments."

Before Kevin can ask, Ruby leans over and hands him a piece. A pencil, too. But it doesn't get him off the hook.

"Mr. Richards, do you recall our policy for coming to class prepared?"

He nods.

"This is the second time this week you've failed to bring appropriate materials. This school is your place of work. Do you expect to have a job when you get older?"

Everyone stares at him. I realize I'm doing it, too. I look down. But not before I see how red his face is getting.

"Yeah." His voice is tight. Controlled.

"What do you think is going to happen to that job if you show up late with none of the things you need to do your work?"

Silence. I look up. Kevin's shoulders rise as he takes a deep breath. "I'll probably lose the job," he says, and starts kicking his heel fast against the leg of his chair.

"You bet you'll lose that job. You need to develop some responsibility."

Kevin stands up so fast the desk tips forward under his legs and crashes to the floor. He's out the door before Mrs. Heath can say anything and halfway down the hall by the time she hollers, "You go straight to the office! I'm calling there now."

She looks back at us. "Are your assignments written down?"

Everybody nods.

"Then open your books and get to work. At the end of class, we'll talk about our Thanksgiving service project."

Mrs. Heath picks up the phone, and the rest of us start reading about Franklin Roosevelt's plan to help people who lost jobs and homes during the Great Depression.

"He was late," she tells the phone. "And his attitude was completely unacceptable."

That's the only side of the story the office will ever hear. Kevin probably won't bother to show up there. Even if he does, even if somebody bothers to listen to him, he won't tell them the truth.

I pick up my binder to get a piece of paper and remember Gianna's note. I glance up at Mrs. Heath's desk.

She's still on the phone. "He should be there by now. I'll fill out a discipline report." She starts typing.

I unfold Gianna's note as quietly as I can and smooth it out over my notebook, like it's a homework assignment.

Hey, Zig!
Happy Halloween!

Underneath, she's sketched a jack-o'-lantern that looks like me. It has floppy black hair and a slightly crooked nose. Underneath that . . .

P.S. Are you going out trick-or-treating tonight?
P.P.S. Are you going to the dance tomorrow?
Just curious. ~G

I look over my shoulder to the corner where she sits. She's looking at me. She must have watched me read her note.

She raises her eyebrows. Question marks.

I look down at her P.S. and P.P.S. And I look back at her and shake my head. She looks at me for a second and then puts her chin down and starts reading her textbook. Or pretending to.

"Mmm-hmm," Mrs. Heath says. "I'd like to arrange a conference with his mother and father."

Good luck, I think as I turn back to my book and FDR's speech about getting the country out of the Great Depression. I like the quote they give from his speech at the 1932 Democratic Convention:

What do the people of America want more than anything else? To my mind, they want two things: work, with all the moral and spiritual values that go with it; and with work, a reasonable measure of security.

Mrs. Heath stands up from her desk and looks at the clock. "I'd like to spend the last ten minutes of class talking about our Thanksgiving service project. We'll be doing something to help the less fortunate."

I don't think I can listen to this. I reach for my pencil to keep working on the questions instead.

"Mr. Zigonski! Care to put down your pencil and listen? This is important."

"Sorry," I say.

She picks up a piece of chalk and points at us with it. "You've been reading about Franklin Roosevelt's New Deal and the Great Depression. But what you might not realize is that there are still many families in our nation living in poverty."

She scribbles a number on the board. "Around two point five million kids in American are homeless. Think about that. Kids like you are living without a place to sleep at night," Mrs. Heath says. "Try to imagine, just for a minute, what that must be like." She pauses.

I don't need to imagine, so I spend my minute looking around. Gianna looks like she's actually thinking about it. Alec

Rayburn is sharpening his pencil, dropping curly shavings all over the floor. Bianca Rinaldi is putting on ChapStick. Ruby is glaring at Mrs. Heath. I wonder if she feels like I do.

When I look at Mrs. Heath up there, though, she doesn't look like a monster. She looks like somebody who doesn't get it. Somebody who thinks poor kids are numbers on her chalkboard instead of real live students without pencils at their desks.

"Now," she says. "Starting at our dance tomorrow night, we'll be collecting canned goods to donate to the food shelf at our local homeless shelter. We'll walk over as a class next week to deliver them."

I feel like somebody just threw a canned good at my head. We're going there on a field trip? To deliver the canned goods. For the poor. For those kids on the blackboard.

"Eww." Bianca Rinaldi wrinkles her nose and raises her hand. "Mrs. Heath, I'm not sure my mother will let me go. That place is full of drunks. I don't think it's safe."

I wait for Mrs. Heath to yell at her. Or send her to the office. Or tell her how stupid she is. She doesn't.

"It's okay, Bianca. We'll be there in the middle of the day. They require clients to be out looking for jobs or taking classes toward their GEDs during the day. These are people for whom education hasn't always been a priority."

The chicken nuggets I ate for lunch feel like they've turned to stone in my stomach. How could she say that? My mother is probably half asleep over her nursing books right now, studying so she can pass her finals in December and get a job so we can have a place again. She told me the other night she found a nice apartment. A great one close to school. But we have to wait and hope it's still available when we can afford it.

"That's not how it is." The words fly from my mouth before I can think.

"Oh?" Mrs. Heath raises her eyebrows. I'm a good student— I still have that reputation from the days when I showed up with pencils and finished homework—so she doesn't yell at me. "Go on, Mr. Zigonski."

"Some people there are educated and want to work. They're going to college. Or trying to find a job. Trying to take care of their kids. They're not all like Brother Vinnie."

Alec Rayburn snickers in the back row, but I keep talking. "You talk about them like they're stupid because they're in a bad situation, and they're not."

Mrs. Heath tips her head and looks interested. "Have you volunteered at the shelter?"

My neck feels hot, and my chest is tight. I feel myself nod.

Mrs. Heath smiles. "What a great experience. We'll have to hear more about that another time."

The bell rings. I'm the first one out.

I don't go to computer class, where I'm supposed to be next. I walk out the school's side door. Let them write me another discipline referral. Let them mail it home with an invitation to schedule a parent conference. Good luck.

I sit in the park for the last hour of school. I can't go to the library or the librarians will ask why I'm not in school.

I pick up a perfectly round pebble and hold it in the palm of my hand. It's warm from the sun and stays warm, like it has a little heater inside.

I try to think back, to remember how many times I've sat in classrooms where we talked about helping the less fortunate and didn't even think about it. I wonder how many kids next to me were squirming. Guys like Kevin.

A heron flies over, fighting the wind, and I think about Ruby. Ruby gets it, even though she doesn't know about Mom and me right now. I really do need to go to her meeting for the herons at city hall on Monday.

Up the street, I can see cars start to spill out of the school parking lot for the end of the day. I stand up, brush off my jeans, and drop my rock. Then I pick it up again.

The lake's pretty calm today. I close my eyes and wish for the food collection project to go away. I wish for Kevin to somehow not get in trouble when he goes back to school. I wish for Mrs. Heath to shut up.

I wish for Dad.

I wrap my fingers around the stone, curl up my arm and fling it out at the perfect angle.

Not even a single skip.

CHAPTER 31
Trick or Treat

"I can't babysit Scoop Monday night," I tell Mom. "I promised Ruby I'd help her with something."

"What are you doing? And why does it have to be at night?" Mom pulls her hair into a ponytail and tightens it. She turns back to her bunk for her apron. "Help her after school instead, and you can be back here by five o'clock."

I shake my head. "I told her I'd go to this meeting at city hall. About the herons."

Mom whips around and drops her apron on the floor. "What?" she says.

"It's a meeting about the herons." I pick up her apron, and she ties it around her waist, but her eyes don't leave me. "Ruby's in Birds First, and I guess some jerks bought up a bunch of land on Smugglers Island to build condominiums for rich people. They want to wipe out a whole heron rookery to do it."

"No." Mom tucks her order pad in her apron pocket and picks up her truck keys.

"Well, I know," I say. "Ruby says there's no way they should be allowed to do that just because the city already approved their zoning request. When that happened, the herons weren't even there yet, but now they are, so—"

"No. Not that. No, you're not going."

"Why?"

"Because . . . because that meeting's downtown, and it's likely to go late." She turns away.

"Seriously?" I move between her and the door so she has to look at me. "I've been walking all over town on my own. Why are you so concerned all of a sudden?"

"Enough." Her eyes challenge me to argue, but today, I'm not up for it. I take the bunk ladder in two steps and flop down.

"Fine," I say.

Mom walks out. Scoop catches the door and walks in with his mom behind him.

"Thank you so much," Heather says, and hands me up a plastic bag full of fur.

"What's this?" I ask.

"It's his lion costume." She scratches Scoop on the top of his head, and he lets out a roar.

"What are you going to be?" he asks. "When we go trick-or-treating?"

Trick-or-treating.

I look up at his mom. "I'm really, really sorry," I say, "I can still babysit, but I have a ton of homework, so I can't go out. I'll need to stay here with him. I honestly can't . . ."

Scoop's eyes fill and he turns to his mom. "You promised."

She looks up at me holding the bag of lion. Her eyes are begging me to go. I nod. "Okay. A few houses."

Half an hour later, Scoop is almost ready. His tail keeps falling off, though, no matter how many times I Velcro it back on.

"Sorry," he says. "It's an old costume my mom got from a lady whose kid is all grown up and moved to Ohio and works at a bank now."

"Hold still." I rip a piece of duct tape from the roll I keep in my backpack and stick his tail back on.

He wiggles, and the tail flops back and forth, but it stays on. "Hey, Zig? I think I might want to work in a bank."

"How come?"

"Because you'd never ever have to worry about money. Banks have tons of money. If you needed to buy a house or something, you could bring some money home from work."

"It doesn't work that way."

"Oh." He picks up his tail and studies the tassel at the end. It's unraveling. "I was just kind of hoping."

We leave the shelter—Scoop dressed as a lion and me wearing a box we found out back and painted really quickly to look like a nine-volt battery. Scoop starts to head for the expensive houses on Dahlia Circle.

"Not there," I say, turning him around. Bianca Rinaldi lives down there. So does our superintendent. No way.

"Why not? They always have the best candy."

"Just . . . because. You're lucky we even came tonight."

A minivan pulls up to the curb. The mom waits behind the wheel while two witches, a football player, the Incredible Hulk, and a doughnut climb out.

"Well, where *can* we go?" Scoop asks. "How about up Washington Street? My old neighbor lives there and she makes cookies."

"Nope." Washington Street would mean Ruby's house, my old apartment, and Gianna's house, all in about three blocks. "We'll go down here." I steer him down Stetson Avenue, which I know from my old paper route. It only has a few houses, and most are old people with no kids.

I look at my watch as Scoop goes up the first set of steps. 7:15. He goes to bed at 8. That means I only have to keep him out another fifteen minutes, so there's time to get ready and read and stuff.

"Trick or treat!" Scoop hollers at an old lady who answers the door.

"Well, aren't you the cutest little bugger?" He roars, and she loads him up with a handful of candy. Maybe we'll be done sooner than I thought.

In the streetlight, I see three kids heading our way. *Don't let them be from here*, I think. *Don't let me know them.* There's a tall one that looks like a girl in a princess dress, another tall guy with paint splattered on his clothes, and a short round kid dressed all in green.

"Come on!" Scoop calls. "Let's go to the next house."

I climb the steps behind him holding his tail so he doesn't trip over it.

"Trick or treat!"

"Well there! Look at you, Mr. Lion!" It's Mr. Benson, who I used to see on my paper route. He'd be up at 5 a.m., watching for me at the window with his coffee so he could open the door and get the paper right from my hand. "Betty! You have to come here and see this little lion!"

Scoop smiles. "I'll roar for her."

Mr. Benson looks past me. "And look what we have here! Wait—don't tell me . . . a princess and . . . a tennis ball? And let's see . . . you would be?"

"Jackson Pollock. The artist."

I recognize her voice, and I want to disappear. But I know I'll have to turn around eventually, so I get it over with. "Hey, Gianna."

"Hey." Her mouth turns down a little. "I thought you weren't going out tonight."

"I wasn't." I look down at Scoop, trying to tear open a Twix bar wrapper with his lion paws. Finally, he just bites it. "But I had to take . . . my cousin out."

Scoop looks up at me, confused. Thankfully, he can't say anything through his mouthful of Twix.

"I thought your aunt Becka didn't have kids," Gianna says, watching him chew.

"She doesn't. He's . . . my dad's brother's kid."

"Your dad has a brother?"

"Not a brother-brother, but a really close friend who's . . . like a brother."

"Oh." She steps up past me. "Trick or treat."

Ruby the princess is behind her. "Hi," she says.

"Hi."

I look down at Ian, Gianna's little brother. He loves Ruby and always insists on holding her hand instead of Gianna's when they take him places. "Nice tennis ball outfit," I tell him.

"I'm not a tennis ball. I'm a pea." He points to Ruby. "Get it? The princess and the pea?" He leans in and whispers to me. "Actually, I thought it would be funnier if I dressed up like a toilet. Then we'd be the princess and the pee—like P-E-E. The princess and the pee? Get it?" He laughs so hard he doubles over. Finally, he stands up again. "But Mom said no."

I nod. "Moms are like that."

Ian and Ruby step forward for their mini chocolate bars, and we end up all walking down the driveway together. Gianna won't look at me. She keeps picking at the paint splashed on her overalls. Little flakes drift down in the streetlight.

"Hey, Gianna," I say. "I really didn't think I was coming out tonight. I hadn't planned on it, so when you asked, I—"

I step toward her, but she holds up her paintbrush to stop me. "It's fine," she says. She says the "fine" part so loud I know it's not.

"Okay. See you Monday."

"Fine." She takes Ian's hand and pulls him down the street.

"I like that guy," Scoop says.

"Ian? Yeah, you would like him. You two are a lot alike."

"Do you like him?" Scoop pulls a Tootsie Roll from his bag, and I help him unwrap it.

"Yeah, I do."

"And you *really* like her."

"We're friends."

"Remember when I asked you if you had a girlfriend and you said no and I said I didn't believe you?"

"Yeah. Hey—got any Starbursts in there?" He hands me one as we start walking back to the shelter.

"Know what?" he says.

"What?"

"I still don't believe you and I think that's the girl that you say isn't your girlfriend but who really is. That Gianna girl."

"Yeah?"

"Yeah. Can you open this for me, too?" He pulls out a little bag of M&M's.

"This is the last one. You have to go to bed soon."

"Okay." He dumps all the M&M's into his paw and shoves them into his mouth.

"Know what else?" he says, chewing as we walk up the shelter steps.

"What?"

"She's mad at you."

"I know." I hold the door for him. "Go get ready for bed. I'll guard your candy while you brush your teeth and change into pajamas."

I hop up on my bunk and wait for him. Gianna's mad all right. And there's nothing I can do about it. When we get out of here, maybe I'll tell her why I acted so dumb. When Mom and I get our new place.

I pull Dad's journal from under my mattress. All those geocaches, and I still have no clue where he is. Not even a dumb phone number or an e-mail address. I check the geocaching website at the library every afternoon to see if he's posted anything new, but he hasn't.

"All set." Scoop gets into his bed, and I toss down his bag of candy.

"Don't eat any more now. You brushed your teeth."

I lean back on my pillow. Maybe Dad's been away on a longer business trip. Maybe when he's back he'll call. Or at least post something on the website so I can get in touch with him. He'd know what to do about this whole Gianna thing.

"Hey, Zig?"

"Yeah?"

"Wanna know one more thing?"

"Sure."

"You ought to tell her you like her. I bet then she wouldn't be mad."

"It's not that simple."

"I figured. I was just hoping. Good night."

"You gotta quit hoping all the time," I say. "Some things are complicated and crummy. G'night." I push the little green journal back under my mattress and try to sleep.

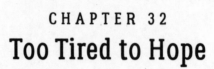

CHAPTER 32
Too Tired to Hope

On Saturday, I hop on my bike and set off to look for the last geocache that Dad logged on the website. It's next to a drainage pipe by the road that leads to the hospital. There's no log book. There's no Canada key chain. No note that says, "Hey, Circuit Boy! Got your last message and I'll be calling soon." Nothing but a Tupperware container packed with two dozen Smurfs. They smile up at me with stupid blue plastic faces that make me want to throw them under a truck.

Instead, I snap them back into their Tupperware and hope they suffocate. I sit down on the drainage pipe, feel the damp, cold moss seep through my jeans, and scroll through the GPS entries, through all the coordinates I thought would lead me to Dad.

All places on a globe. None of them the right one.

My sneakers squish the soft earth when I jump down from

the pipe and get on my bike to ride back to the shelter. Maybe you just can't find someone who doesn't want to be found.

When I get back, everyone's in the dinner line except Scoop. He's waiting at the door.

"Darn," he says. "You're here."

"Thanks for the warm welcome," I say.

"I was hoping you went to that dance with your girlfriend."

"She's not my girlfriend."

"Fine." He gets in line and hands me a packet of silverware. "But I still don't believe you."

"Fine." I take a serving of macaroni and cheese, even though the top looks kind of burned.

"And you know what?"

"What?" I say, adding wilted lettuce to my plate.

"You should have gone."

Mom's working Sunday, but Heather isn't, so nobody harasses me to take care of Scoop, which is good. I need a break.

Mom hands me a box of cornflakes and gathers her nursing books into her bag. "It's apple pie day at the diner. Want to come by later?"

I shrug.

"You should bring Gianna and Ruby. I haven't seen them in a while."

"They're busy."

"What are you doing today, then?"

"Geez, Mom. Does it matter?" I snap.

She stops and turns to me. "Don't say that."

"Does it?" I say again. Mom looks at her watch. She has to leave for work, but I don't care. "We've been here a month, Mom. A *month*. You said it was going to be a few days." My eyes burn. I wipe them with the back of my sweatshirt sleeve. "And you *still* won't call Dad to ask for help. I've done everything except take out an ad in the newspaper to find him, and I'm tired of this."

"Kirby . . . you don't—"

"Don't tell me I don't understand because I understand fine. I'm tired of living down the hall from a bunch of creeps who steal my stuff and try to get me to buy it back from them. I'm tired of being a free babysitter for your friend. I'm tired of hoping. I'm tired of everything." I slam the cereal box on the nightstand. Cornflakes fly out the top.

Mom brushes them into her hand. It's red and chapped.

"You've been looking for him?" she says.

I nod and feel the tears spill down my face.

"How?"

I pull the GPS unit from my backpack. "His geocaches. They're all logged on a website. I've been going on the library computers after school."

Mom shakes her head. "He hasn't geocached in a long time, Kirb."

"June fifth." I turn the dial to get to Dad's last set of coordinates. "This was the last one."

She takes the GPS unit and scrolls through my list. When she gets to the end, she looks up and hands it back to me. "I'm sorry," she says.

"Now will you call him?"

She looks at me for a long time. Then she shakes her head. "I can't. And stop looking. You're not going to find him. I'm sorry. And I'm sorry I'm not giving you answers right now. I know how frustrated you are, and I promise, pretty soon you'll understand why he can't help but until then, please . . . let it go." She looks at her watch. "I have to go to work. I'm late."

I stare at her.

"I need to go. Okay?"

"No." It's not okay. None of it is.

"What are you going to do today? Would you go to Gianna's or something, please? I hate the idea of you wandering around."

"I'm going for a walk." And I leave.

When I get to the corner, I look back. Mom's standing there on the sidewalk in front of the shelter. Finally, she walks off in the direction of the diner.

When she's out of sight, I go back to the shelter. Back to room five and the bag I've kept under my mattress. I spill it out on the wool blanket. The Canada key chain. The Florida State quarter. The Martin Luther quote. The headless army guy. The piece of marble.

The journal. I shove it all into my backpack, get on my bike, and leave.

All day, I follow the black arrows. 0.68 miles. 123 yards. 39 yards. 12 yards. 3 yards.

I follow them to the leaf pile under the tree.

The bushes near the river.

The footbridge.

The drainage pipe by the hospital.

I put everything back. It was so stupid. All of it.

Finally, I follow the coordinates to the train tracks by the lake. The sky's been November gray all day, and now it's starting to rain. A crummy fall rain with big wet cold drops.

I sit down on a railroad tie and watch them plunking in the water. I tuck the journal under my sweatshirt to keep it dry. I don't know why I bother. The rain gets harder and harder until it looks like the lake is boiling.

I shove the journal into the rocks where I found it and head toward the marina.

That heron—at least it looks like the same one—is standing at the end of the dock again. In the pouring rain. Stupid bird. It can't be fishing—it couldn't see anything with the water all churned up. But it watches the surface. Waiting. For the longest time.

Then it plunges its head into the water and comes up with a perch flopping in its beak. I guess there's always hope if you hang around long enough.

I look back at the railroad tracks. The rain is coming down hard. And I didn't shove the journal in very far.

The wet railroad ties are old and slippery. But I step from

one rough-hewn log to another until I get back to the spot. I lay down on the tracks and reach until I feel the rough cover of the journal.

It's only a little damp. I wipe it on my jeans, tuck it back into my jacket, and head back to the marina.

The heron is still on the dock, gulping down its dinner.

And all of a sudden, I'm hungry, too.

When I get back to the shelter and lock up my bike, it's dark. The kind of dark that doesn't seem like a big deal when you're outside, but when you go in, it looks pitch-black out the window, so you understand why people were wondering where you were.

"Your mom was getting ready to send out the troops," Rob Thomas says when I sit down at one of the dining tables with my sandwich and carrot sticks. "She's getting changed from work." He puts down his newspaper and raises his eyebrows at my dripping hair and soggy sweatshirt. "Looks like you've had a rough day."

"No rougher than usual," I say. I look down at the Sunday paper and catch the headline on the front page.

**Smugglers Island Heron Controversy
Spawns Protest
Demonstration Planned for City Council Meeting**

"Can I borrow this?"

He nods and I pull the paper over so I can read while I eat.

A hand swoops in and snatches it away from me.

"Hey! I was reading that."

But Mom folds the paper up in such a tight little roll you can't even see the headline anymore. "Heather needs it to look for apartments," she says, and tucks it under her arm.

"Not in the news section. Give her classifieds and let me have that. It has a story about Ruby's heron meeting."

Mom keeps the paper under her arm. "You're not going to that meeting. It's a school night."

I start to argue but remember that she's working tomorrow night. I'll be able to do whatever I want. I don't need the dumb paper when I can go to the meeting.

"Okay," I say.

She looks surprised. "Okay?"

I nod. "Okay."

She breathes out and closes her eyes, like me not being out on a school night tomorrow is the most important thing in the world. But she doesn't say anything about the fact that I'm soaking wet and was out past dark. Maybe Mom's tired of everything, like me. Too tired to care.

"Good night," I tell her.

She kisses me on the cheek. "I'm going to study. I'll be a couple hours."

I finish my sandwich, toss my trash, change into dry clothes, and head into room five. Heather and Scoop are crammed into Scoop's bed, both asleep with *Library Lion* flopped open across their laps.

I climb carefully into my bunk and take out Dad's journal. It's still damp.

I flip through the pages, through the raindrop smears. Then I tuck it back under my mattress. Just in case.

CHAPTER 33
Pencil Problems

"Mr. Zigonski?"

I look up from my social studies textbook and see Mrs. Heath at her desk, peering over her glasses. She curls her finger at me to come up.

"Mr. Zigonski, you realize that you have four late homeworks this quarter?"

"Sorry."

"Sorry is not an excuse. Is your assignment for today done?"

"I was finishing it. I couldn't find a pencil last night."

She takes off her glasses and huffs, as if I've insulted her personally. "Homework is to be done at home. Are you suggesting to me that there's not a pencil to be found in your entire house?"

I don't say anything. I have no idea what's in the house

where I used to live. I'd imagine somebody new lives there by now. Somebody with rent money. Probably pencils, too.

"Your grade has gone from an A to a B-minus since last quarter."

I nod. I'm surprised it's not lower. Mom's been busy every night studying or working. I've been helping with dinners, babysitting for Scoop. Sometimes I get homework done in the library at lunch, but lately there hasn't been enough time, even though Mr. Smythe always leaves pencils out for me now.

Mrs. Heath taps her red pen on my name in her grade book. "Report cards are mailed home soon. I'm going to include a note for your mother and father about scheduling a conference with me." She looks at me.

"Okay."

Go for it, Mrs. Heath. Knock yourself out, I think. *I'll be extra impressed if you find my dad.* I start back to my seat.

"And Mr. Zigonski?"

I turn back to her.

"You realize you haven't brought in any canned goods for the food drive?" She nods at the mountain that's accumulated in the corner. Cans of corn and peas. Boxes of pasta and cereal. Somebody brought in eight huge cans of beets. Jars of peanut butter.

"That's worth extra credit," Mrs. Heath says. "It would help right about now."

I nod. "Sure thing."

"Don't forget—" She raises her voice, as if everyone in the class wasn't just listening to her lecture me about my B-minus. "And this is for everyone. Tomorrow is the last day to bring in food to help the needy. We'll be walking up to the homeless shelter right after this period to deliver it."

When the last bell rings, I grab my stuff from my locker and rush to the front door to wait for Gianna. I tried to talk to her in English, but she wouldn't even look at me. I can't believe she'd be that mad about a dumb dance. But I know she'll be happy when I tell her and Ruby I'm coming to the meeting tonight.

"Hey, Zigonski!" Kevin Richards shuffles down the hall toward me. He lowers his voice. "You doing okay?"

I stare at him. Waiting for the punch line. With Richards, that could be literal. Sometimes, he'll tell a dumb joke and then clobber you if you don't laugh. But he just stands there, waiting for me to answer.

"I'm okay. Why?"

"Just checking. I haven't seen you around." He looks around. "And I know it's hard the first time. It even freaked me out, so I figured that you . . ."

"That I'm so much of a wimp I'd never be able to handle it?"

"Well, yeah." He smiles.

"I'm okay," I say. Ruby and Gianna are coming down the hall, almost tripping over each other because they're reading something between them. "I gotta go." I step aside and head over to meet them.

Gianna sees me first, elbows Ruby, grabs what turns out to be a newspaper, and shoves it into her backpack over her shoulder as I approach.

Ruby steps in front of her. "Hey," she says.

"Hey. All ready for your meeting tonight?"

She hands me a flyer. "We've been putting these up all over."

THEY WERE HERE FIRST

Save Rookery Bay!
Make your voice heard at the Lakeland City Council
Meeting—Monday, November 3.

At the bottom, there's an incredible drawing of a great blue heron in flight.

"Wow, Gee! This is awesome." I lean around Ruby to see her.

"Thanks. It didn't photocopy well, but it's okay." She looks in a hurry to leave, and I can't tell if she's still mad about the dance. There are leftover posters up all over the front hallway. "$3 admission! Live DJ! Loads of fun!" says the one next to me.

"Listen, I really couldn't go on Saturday," I say.

"It's fine," she says quickly. "I ended up babysitting for my little brother anyway."

"Really? I thought you were excited because it was the first dance of the year."

She looks at Ruby, rolls her eyes, and walks off.

I hand Ruby back the poster and follow her out the front door, down the steps. "What's her problem?"

"Just that the smartest boy in the school is also the dumbest boy in the school."

"Me?"

"She likes you. *Likes* you, likes you. You know that, right?"

"Well . . . I guess . . . I didn't really . . ." I watch Gianna power walking away from us, toward the park. "She *likes* me, likes me?"

Ruby nods. "She waited forever for you to ask her to that stupid dance, and then you didn't, so then she finally got up the nerve to ask if you were going, and you blew her off. Why couldn't you show up at the dumb dance? You could have at least gone with her as a friend." Now Ruby seems mad, too.

"I'm going to that meeting with you guys tonight," I offer.

Ruby's eyes get big for a second. Then she says. "No. Don't do that. I mean, don't bother. I know you've been busy. It's okay."

"But I want to." I walk faster, hoping we'll catch up with Gee. "I agree with you about the birds. Those guys have to be jerks to think about cutting down the trees where the herons nest. If they think—"

Ruby stops and whirls around to face me. "You can't go."

"Why not?"

"Because . . . everybody who's speaking had to sign up with the city council in advance. It's too late."

"I don't have to speak. I can—"

"We're all set. Seriously. There are plenty of people coming. My mom and my aunt. Mr. Webster from the park. A bunch of people from school. Gianna's going to talk, and she'll be all nervous if you're there, so just . . . don't. Please?"

I look ahead to the park, expecting to see Gee waiting. But she didn't stop.

"She's really mad, huh?" We start walking again.

Ruby sighs. "She's sad and confused and mad, yes. There's kind of a lot going on right now. But you guys will figure things out. Be honest with her."

Be honest. Like that's the easiest thing ever.

We stop at the park. At least, I do.

Ruby keeps walking. "I'll see you tomorrow," she calls over her shoulder.

"You're not stopping to skip rocks?"

"Too much to do. But I'll see you tomorrow. And we have that field trip, remember?"

How could I forget? That field trip to the homeless shelter. To deliver food to the less fortunate. Like me.

CHAPTER 34
No More Secrets

"I brought corn. I love canned corn," Gianna says, pulling her jacket closed.

As we walk to the shelter with Mrs. Heath's class, it's one of those mornings when fall and winter overlap. There are still leaves on some trees, and a few let go with every gust of wind. It's snowing, too. Not the good, fluffy flakes. Just little scraps of white that spit down mixed with rain and sleet.

Ruby's walking on one side of me, Gianna on the other. They don't seem mad anymore. All they said about the meeting last night is that it was fine. Lots of people showed up to support the herons. It was fine that I didn't go.

I should have stayed home today, too. Well, not home . . . but I should have skipped out somewhere. Kevin had the right idea. He's absent. Probably hanging out at some pizza place instead of delivering canned goods to his own kitchen.

Gianna's plastic grocery bag full of corn clanks against my bag, with the one can of tuna fish I swiped from the shelter kitchen this morning. It was actually sitting out on the table where I sit at breakfast, like somebody left it there. I didn't ask. I just took it. I figure it's not stealing. That tuna's going right back where it came from.

And here we are. My bike is locked to the rack out front. What if Gianna recognizes it? I swallow hard. At least I know nobody staying here will be around because of the leave-by-eight rule. But Rob Thomas will be here. I pull up my sweatshirt hood and try to work my way into the middle of the group. I'm counting on him being too busy to pay much attention to a bunch of middle school kids and their canned corn.

"Now, students . . ." Mrs. Heath stops at the front of the line so we all bunch up like a kid-accordion. "Before we go in, I want to remind you of your manners. Just because someone is homeless doesn't mean they don't have feelings, so—"

"I thought you said none of the homeless people would be here," Bianca says.

"Bianca, enough," Mrs. Heath says. "There aren't likely to be any people here now who are staying at the shelter, but even if there were, I'd expect you to be polite." She looks down at the clipboard she's holding in her black leather gloves. "We're meeting a Mr. Thomas, and he'll let us know where to put these things. Then we'll all get together with the pile of food and take a picture for the yearbook."

I fall back into the middle of the line and keep my head down as we shuffle through the door. My chest is so tight it feels like someone's sitting on it. I force myself to take a deep breath. Bianca turns around. It must have been a noisy breath.

"What's wrong?" she says as we walk down the hallway with its light green walls. We stop and wait for Mrs. Heath to talk with an office person.

"Sorry," I say. "Just nervous."

Bianca nods. "I know. Isn't it kind of freaky being in here? It creeps me out, even if the people aren't here, you know?"

I don't say anything. I drift farther back in the line so I'm behind Max Hayes. He's huge and on the football team. A good hiding-behind guy.

"Okay, students," Mrs. Heath calls from the front of our line. "I want you to meet Rob Thomas. He's been with the shelter for twelve years. He's the person who helps to get new people settled here when they need a place to stay. He'll be taking our donations."

"Thanks so much for coming," he says. "We appreciate your donations, but mostly, we appreciate your willingness to walk through these doors." He walks down our line of kids as he talks. "I know I recognize a few of you from our volunteer food service program, since you've visited to help serve dinners." He nods at Ruby. Great. One more thing to worry about. "But many of you have probably never been here before. Some of you might even be a little nervous."

As he gets closer to my part of the line, I turn around and

pretend to look at one of the announcements on the bulletin board behind me.

"But now that you're here," he says, "I think you'll see this is a pretty normal place. Maybe more crowded than your house, but certainly a place where you'd be welcome if your family were ever in trouble."

"Fat chance," whispers Bianca.

Rob either doesn't hear her, or ignores her. "And I hope you'll realize that our clients are regular people. Kids, some of them. Kids who do homework, and watch TV, and want to grow up and follow dreams, just like you. Our job is to help them through the rough times."

I hear his footsteps pass me and move away, so I turn back around.

"Come on over here," he says, "and you can leave your donations in our kitchen."

"We'll need a photo for the yearbook," Mrs. Heath says.

Rob shakes his head. "I'm sorry, but we don't allow any photographs to be taken in the shelter. This is our clients' home, albeit a temporary one. And I'm sure you wouldn't want strangers taking pictures in your home while you were out for the day."

"Of course," Mrs. Heath says, but she doesn't look happy about it.

"Okay, kids, you can circle through the dining room and come back here," Rob says as the line starts moving. "That way, I can say thanks personally on your way out."

I look back at the door. Is there time for me to duck out-side? I could hand my canned tuna off to somebody and say I need to use the bathroom. Or that I feel sick. That would be true enough. But it would draw more attention, and the line's already shuffling me forward into the kitchen. I wish I had skipped a stone at the park yesterday and it had gone ten times. I'd wish to be invisible.

I shuffle forward and plunk my can of tuna fish on the coun-ter. The cornflakes I had for breakfast are sitting by the cup-board next to the sink.

I walk through the dining room, following Max between the tables. My chair—the one I always sit in—is pushed out a little. I push it in.

And then the line stops. Because Rob Thomas is at the front.

"It's great to meet you," he says, shaking Ronald Boyer's hand. "Thanks for your donation today and for taking the time to visit."

The line inches forward. Maybe I should slip back to the very end, so everyone else will be gone by the time I get to Rob. I look back to see how many people are behind me. Just six. But the last two are Ruby and Gianna. They'd wait for me for sure. Why couldn't they still be mad? Then they could stomp off and leave me alone.

Every time the line moves, I take two more baby steps for-ward, and the vise that's clenched around my stomach gets tighter. Finally, Max Hayes steps up.

"Hi! What's your name?" Rob asks.

"Max Hayes."

"Max, you play football, right? I think I saw you play against my son's school last weekend."

Max nods.

"Great game," Rob says. "Thanks for coming today."

Max goes to wait in the hallway.

I take a deep breath and look up at Rob. He doesn't look surprised to see me.

"Hi there," he says. "What's your name?"

I stare at him for a second before I figure it out.

He knows me. He's just not telling.

He gets it.

I'm saved.

"Uh . . . Kirby," I say.

He reaches out to shake my hand. "Kirby, it's great to meet you. Thanks for your donation today."

I nod, and he nods, and I step over next to Max and almost collapse against the wall, I'm so relieved. I stare up at the ceiling while Rob greets the rest of the line.

"Hi, Dylan. Thanks for your donation. It's a great help to us."

"Hey, Ryan. I'm glad you came to visit."

"Ruby and Gianna, good to meet you. Thanks for coming today."

"Okay, class," says Mrs. Heath. "We're going to head out now. Make a line, and we'll stop at the corner."

I look back. Rob nods at me the slightest bit, and everything makes sense.

The tuna fish left on the counter this morning.

He knows I'm in eighth grade. He knew the eighth graders were donating food today.

Rob's done this before. He has bunches of classes come with donations every year, and every year, some of those kids must be clients. He keeps their secrets.

My secret.

The first person in our line opens the door, and the cool November air spills in. It feels like a cold drink of water on a hot day. I can't wait to get back outside.

But then the line moves back a little. Whoever's in front had to step away from the door to let somebody in.

"It's people who *live* here," Bianca whispers, back to the rest of the line.

Rob steps to the front to meet the people coming in. I can't see over Max's head, but I hear Heather's voice.

"I'm so sorry. I forgot that Scoop had a doctor's appointment this morning, and I need to pick up my insurance paperwork. We'll just be a minute, and then we won't be back until the regular time."

"No problem, come on in."

Our class line starts heading out. When I figure Heather and Scoop must be gone down the hallway, I lift my head to look.

"Zig?"

I duck and try to walk forward, but Max is hard to get past.

"Hey, Zig! What are you doing here now? Are these the kids in your class? Is your girlfriend here? Hey, Zig! After dinner tonight, will you play Sorry with me?"

"You *know* them?" Bianca's eyes are huge.

I could pretend I don't. I could pretend he's some random homeless kid.

But he's not. He's Scoop.

I step out of line and give him a hug. "Yeah, we'll play tonight. Right after dinner."

"Cool!" He waves and runs down the hall after Heather.

Max and Bianca and the rest of the line are out the door now. The whole line, except me. And Ruby and Gianna. They're staring at me.

"You didn't tell me," Gianna whispers.

There's nothing I can say except the truth.

"You're right. I didn't."

CHAPTER 35
Holding On

I can't look at Gianna all day.

At lunch, I grab my sandwich and hide in the library. Mr. Smythe leaves a pencil and extra paper for me every day now. He never asked if I needed them; he just knew. If he had asked, I'd have told him no, I was fine. Maybe he knew that, too.

I try to solve equations, but they all remind me of Mom's checkbook. I doodle bricks around the edges of my paper instead.

When lunch ends, I go to my other classes and finally, the last bell rings. I poke around in my locker, rearranging binders until I'm sure Gianna and Ruby are gone.

When I walk past the park, I expect an ambush, but they're not waiting.

I sit down on the swing and turn, twisting the chains into a tangle that looks the way I feel.

I knew it would wreck everything. I knew Gianna wouldn't understand. She doesn't get it. How can you, when you go home to your house with your mom and dad both there, with your dad actually working and paying bills, and your mom home to make sure there's broccoli or something with dinner and not just macaroni and cheese served up by a church lady.

"Are you using that?" A little kid in a puffy blue coat points to my second swing.

"No, go ahead." I let it go.

He jumps on and wiggles himself into the middle of the swing. "Ready, Dad! Push me high!"

Two big hands grab the bottom of the swing on both sides, lift it high into the air, and let go.

"I can see the roof of the library!" the boy calls before he sinks back down again. His dad stands behind him and keeps pushing so he doesn't lose altitude.

"Higher, Dad!" The dad lets go for a second to button a couple buttons on his jacket. He pushes up his glasses and reaches out to push again.

I stand up and start for the sidewalk.

"Hey, did you want a push?" the kid calls after me. "'Cause my dad will push you, too, if you want."

"No, thanks," I say. "I have to go somewhere."

I climb the library steps, swing the door open, and wave to the front desk lady. She nods me toward the open computer. The one I checked every day until last week.

I type in the geocaching URL and wait for it to load.

There's not going to be anything. I know there's not. But it doesn't matter. I have to check.

I type the words into the website search box: SENIOR SEARCHER.

The list comes up, and I scroll through his found caches, a travel log of my past five weeks. Nest Egg. The Superhero's Lair. Tabletop Cache.

I scroll to the bottom of the list and see it.

High H_2O.

A new cache, with coordinates that put it right here in town.

I'm sure it wasn't listed here last week. My heart pounds in my ears as I click on the cache name for details. And I see the date: November 3.

Yesterday.

He was here.

My heart's full of the kind of rush you get when you're a little kid and see your Easter basket full of candy, or money under your pillow from the tooth fairy.

Dad was here.

I fumble with my backpack until I find the GPS unit and enter the coordinates. I check the website for the clue and jot down the code. I'm about to log off when I see a note in the log at the bottom of the cache page.

> *Comment from Senior Searcher . . . Nice hide! Couldn't find this one before it got dark tonight, but I'll be giving it another try first thing Saturday morning. It's a tough one, but Senior Searcher hasn't failed yet!*

I read it again.

I'll be giving it another try first thing Saturday morning.

He'll be here. My dad will be *here*, at these coordinates on this screen on Saturday morning.

My hands are shaking. I put down the GPS and log off the computer.

"Thanks!" I call to Miss Light, the librarian. She waves as I fly out the door and bound down the steps two at a time.

I have to go now. I know he won't be there until Saturday, but I need to see this cache now. I'll leave him a note. I pull out a pencil and scribble on the back of my social studies homework as I walk.

> Senior Searcher:
> PLEASE don't leave Saturday without seeing me. I have your journal.
> ~Circuit Boy

The GPS unit points southeast, so I head back toward school. Past the football field. Past the big houses on Dahlia Circle. Past the shelter and south.

When I get to the trailer park by the river, it points to a left turn, only there's no street or sidewalk to turn down. Just an empty field where the old water tower stands.

My sneakers squish in the wet grass. My toes are freezing, but I barely notice. The numbers on the GPS unit count down. 54 yards. 48 yards. 36 yards. I'm headed straight for the water tower.

When I walk up to it, the unit says I'm four yards away.

Four yards away from what? I search the ground, looking for a Tupperware container, but there's nothing. And there's really nowhere to hide a cache here. It's all dead grass around the tower.

Then I spot the ladder. It's not a regular ladder that starts at the ground and goes up. This one starts about five feet off the ground and leads all the way to the storage tank at the top of the tower, maybe sixty feet over my head. I reach up to see if the ladder pulls down but it doesn't. There must be a lower part that the city workers used to bring when they came here to do maintenance.

But the city uses a different reservoir now. The tower is empty, so nobody goes up there anymore.

Almost nobody.

I drop my backpack on the ground. My note for Dad blows out of an unzipped pocket, and I have to chase it down. I find a good-sized rock and weight it down right next to the ladder so he'll find it when he comes in the morning.

But I still want to find the cache. I want to find it first.

I zip the GPS unit in my jacket pocket and reach for the bottom rung of the ladder.

Now I know why they make you do those pull-ups in gym class. Mr. Teeter said someday I'd be thankful to him for making me practice, and he was right.

I pull myself up and start climbing. The ladder groans when I take the fifth step, and I stop. My hands are already scratched and rusty from holding the cold metal rungs. I test the sixth step with one foot. It feels plenty sturdy, so I step.

Step by slow step, I climb the tower.

Look. Step. Creak.

Look. Step. Creak.

Finally, my hand touches the railing on the catwalk that goes all around the middle of the tank. This must be where the cache is hidden. It makes sense when I remember the clue: High H_2O. That's the chemical formula for a water molecule, and this tower is definitely high.

I pull myself onto the catwalk and stand up to look for the cache, but the sun, low in the sky, catches me right in the face.

I squint into the warm rays, shining through the clouds, and for the first time in weeks, I feel great. Like everything's finally going to be okay again.

I work my way around the edge of the catwalk. I check along the wall, even underneath the railing in case somebody taped a film canister there. I make a full circle, but there's nothing. No wonder Dad had such a hard time finding this one.

The sun is lower now, turning the sky all kinds of purple-red. I finally give up, lower myself onto the ladder, and start climbing down.

I'm on my way down, heading home, but already planning to come back. I'll have to wake up super early on Saturday. Dad didn't say what time he was coming.

He'll be surprised to see me here, for sure. I bet he just got back to town and was getting ready to call me anyway. Maybe he's been *trying* to call but lost Mom's cell number and doesn't know where we are.

The sun is down, and the wind's picking up, so I climb faster. Hand, hand. Foot, foot. It's going to be so great to see him.

He'll laugh when he finds me here. That's what he'll do. He'll tip back his head and laugh, right after he gives me a big hug. Then we'll find the cache together, and we'll go back online and put a note on the website that says—

Just as I bring my foot down on the ladder, the rung comes loose. It disappears out from under me, clangs on the one below it, and plummets to the ground. I clutch the rung above me with both hands. The rusty metal scrapes my palms as I dangle. My feet flounder around for another rung.

My left foot catches the rung above the one that broke. I pull myself up, shaking so hard I can barely hold on.

I look down. It must be another forty feet to the ground. That kind of fall could kill you.

When I catch my breath, I try to stretch my foot down to the next rung on the ladder, under the one that broke. I can't reach.

I pull myself back up to the higher rung and look down. The light is fading, but I can make out the broken rung in the dry grass way below.

I stretch down again without letting go to see if I can tell how far I'd have to drop to reach that rung.

And I see lights.

Flashing red and blue lights.

I pull my leg back up.

A police car drives up to the base of the tower. An officer jumps out with a megaphone and slams his door shut.

"This is Officer Perry of the Lakeland Police. You need to stay where you are, okay?"

It's not like I have many options.

"We'll send someone up for you. I repeat, stay where you are and hold on. This water tower is not safe."

No kidding.

As if to underscore his message, two big fire trucks—the long ones with the huge ladders—pull up, along with another police car and an ambulance.

The firefighters spread a big tarp underneath the water tower ladder. I guess that's what I'm supposed to land on if I fall.

Even thinking about that drop makes my stomach wobble. My arms and legs are shaking from holding on. I cling to the ladder and press my cheek against the cold metal in the dark.

The firefighters extend one of the long ladders. A woman climbs up and straps a harness on me so I can't fall. Then we climb down together.

When I get to the bottom, one more vehicle pulls in alongside the rescue vehicles. This one scares me more than the fire trucks and police cars combined.

It's Mom.

CHAPTER 36
Letting Go

"We'll release him into your custody if you can promise us this won't happen again," the cop says.

Mom nods, reaches for my elbow, and pulls me closer. "We can definitely make that promise."

I nod. I feel like an idiot.

"You're a lucky young man." The cop looks at me. He probably thinks I'm some spoiled, bored kid who only climbed up here to mess around.

Lucky.

Yeah.

"Kirby?" Mom nudges me.

"Yes, sir. Thank you."

Mom and I watch the firefighters pack up their bouncy blue tarp and load the ladder back onto the truck. Scoop would think that was the coolest thing ever.

When the police cars and fire trucks are gone, I start for the car, but Mom pulls me back toward the water tower. "Come sit." She plunks down on the dry grass near the base. Right next to the letter I wrote Dad.

She looks down at it. "I figured," she says. She hands me the letter. "Senior Searcher isn't your dad, Kirb."

I stare at her in the murky half darkness. "How do you know?"

"I know."

"But you *don't*. You haven't seen these caches—they're so clever, Mom. They're *so* him. This has to be him. Also, he stopped geocaching this summer until just now. Just now this week. I found an entry in his log online. He's coming back here Saturday to try and find the cache, and I'm coming. I know you don't want to see him or talk to him, but you can't keep me from seeing him. He's my dad. I won't try to climb up there again, but I'm coming here in the morning. I'm going to see him." A tear falls from my face to the paper and smears the ink. I shake it at her. "This is my dad!"

She closes her eyes. "It's not."

"Why do you keep saying that? You don't know!"

"I do know." Her eyes open and look right at me. "Your dad is in federal prison."

I stare at her. Then I stare up at the sky.

An airplane trails across the sky behind the water tower and disappears into the distant trees.

Prison.

Mom sits watching me. Waiting.

But that one word sucks all of my other words out of my brain.

Finally, one comes back.

"Why?"

She moves closer to me and wraps her sweater around her more tightly. Like it will keep the story she's telling out of her heart. "The land deal, Kirb. Your dad was part of the Smugglers Island land deal with some other men."

"And he's in *prison*?"

"At the city council meeting this week, they revoked the zoning permission for the condominiums to be built because it came out that the developers had planned to sabotage the heron colony on the island."

"What? How?"

Mom takes a deep breath. "The nests, Kirby. Months ago, a phone tap caught them discussing a plan to put cooking oil on the eggs in the nests so none of them could hatch. They thought it would make the herons abandon the rookery and move on. To make way for the condos."

"They were going to kill the birds in the eggs?"

Mom nods. "They would have suffocated."

"And Dad was part of that?" I feel sick. The pit I felt in my stomach when the ladder rung gave out was nothing compared to this.

Mom shakes her head. "Dad's friends. They've done this before, Kirb." She reaches into her book bag, pulls out the front page of Sunday's newspaper, and unfolds it. "Here," she says with a rush of breath. I put down my letter to Dad and move the rock back on top. Not that it matters.

I take the newspaper.

His picture is on the front page. I don't know how I didn't see it before, when I glanced at the paper at the shelter before Mom grabbed it. Actually, yeah, I know how. His hair is shorter and slicker. And his mustache is gone. But it's Dad.

The article at the top of the page is about the city council meeting. This one, right below it, has a different headline:

Lakeland Developer Sentenced in Florida

I look up at Mom. "Florida?"

She nods. "Remember Ruby's story that you told me? About the guy who ordered the bald eagle nest destroyed because he thought it'd clear the way for a golf course expansion."

I look down and read.

Kirby Zigonski, Senior, a prominent Lakeland real estate developer who manages properties . throughout the Northeast, has pled guilty to violating protected wildlife laws. Zigonski admitted he hired a landscaper named Robert Jamison to cut down the tree in which Zigonski knew bald eagles were nesting. Zigonski's golf course expansion project had been put on hold by the Lee County Environmental Protection Council because of the presence of the eagle.

Jamison was arrested when a neighbor called police to report him cutting down the tree early on the morning of June 20. Jamison told police that Zigonski had approached him about doing the work and that he himself had no information about the eagle nest in the tree. Jamison was released on his own recognizance, and police charged Zigonski, who was held without bail until last week's court hearing, at which he pleaded guilty and was sentenced to one year in prison.

The bald eagle, which biologists believe to be a six-year-old female, has not returned to the area. Her nest and the two eggs in it were destroyed when the tree fell.

My dad. Such a great, funny guy. The one who shows up with presents and limousines and tells jokes. And kills birds so he can make money.

When I look up from the paper, Mom's leaning back, staring up at the tower.

"He used to be so different, Kirby. So different."

I know. "He used to be fun, didn't he? Before he started only caring about real estate and stuff."

Mom nods. "We used to come here for picnics." A Burger King cheeseburger wrapper rustles past us. "It was beautiful then. Wildflowers all over. We'd spread out a blanket like this, eat our sandwiches, and watch the stars get brighter."

"Was I there?"

"Yeah, you were. You were a baby."

I look up at the stars, poking through the clouds. I want to remember, but I can't.

"Dad always said he'd give you the moon and the stars if he could. And I told him no, we already had everything we needed."

"Guess that wasn't enough, huh?" I pluck a blade of grass and blow on it to whistle, but it's too dry and scratchy.

"No, it wasn't enough." Mom sighs. "I'm not sure anything ever will be."

Gently, she pulls the newspaper from my hand and slides it into her backpack. "I'm sorry. He wanted to tell you about all this himself, and I was going to respect that. He loves you, he really does. He felt like he should explain all this."

"Well, he didn't."

"No. He didn't." She leans back. "He's not strong. Not like you. I don't think he could bring himself to write to you or call you. He won't answer my letters now either."

The wind gusts, and the letter I wrote him flutters and flaps under the rock. I smooth it out. "I really thought this was him."

"You really wanted it to be."

I nod.

"Come on," Mom says. "We should get back." We start walking to the car.

But everything feels so unfinished. I stop. So does she.

"How could you let me . . ." I look up at the water tower, at the ladder I was clinging to half an hour ago. At the hope I was clinging to. And I feel so stupid. "You should have told me."

"I should have," Mom says. "I was hoping. Hoping he'd do the right thing and tell you the truth on his own. Hoping he'd write to you. Hoping things would work out with the apartment. Hoping we'd find a new place. I was doing lots of hoping and not enough of everything else." She turns to me. "When I get my degree next month, I'll start nursing, and we'll be able to move. I promise."

She starts walking again, and I follow. Her backpack makes her shoulders droop. It's probably loaded with books for her classes, like always.

"Everything that is done in the world is done by hope," I say.

Mom pulls keys from her pocket to unlock the truck door. "What's that from?"

"Something I read once," I say. I get in and peer up at the water tower through the windshield.

I was so sure it was him.

CHAPTER 37
A Secret Mission

School passes in a blur the rest of the week. Little things like not having a pencil matter less after you almost get killed hanging off a water tower.

On Saturday morning, I wake up to a loud clunk on the floor. Dad's journal—no, somebody else's journal—has slipped out from under my pillow and fallen off the bunk.

I climb down to pick it up and check my watch. 9:30. It's a weekend, so I could sleep in. Heather and Scoop are gone, and Mom's covering the breakfast shift at the diner until at least ten.

I pick up the journal and open it to a page in the middle.

May 28 . . . It's Memorial Day weekend on the lake, and I am doing far too much remembering on this old dock. This is where I brought L fishing for the first time, taught her how to put a worm on a hook. She was a natural.

I have to stop myself from picturing Mom baiting a hook. This book isn't about her anymore. I turn the page.

> *What's become of those memories?*
>
> *A great blue heron on shore just lunged into the weeds. Until he moved, I hadn't even seen him, though I'm sure he was watching me the whole time. He's lifted his head now, and a frog's hind legs stick out from his beak. That frog probably had all kinds of plans for today. Eating flies. Swimming in the shallows.*
>
> *The heron gulps, and the legs disappear. It lifts its great wings and flies off toward the island. Plans don't always work out.*

"No kidding." I close the journal and turn to climb back into bed.

"No kidding what?" Scoop is standing in the doorway holding a toaster.

"What's that?" I ask him.

"No kidding what? You said no kidding. No kidding what?"

I look down at the journal in my hands. Full of some stranger's words. It's too much to explain.

"I don't know."

"Did you ever find your dad?" he asks, sitting down on his bunk with the toaster in his lap.

"No."

"Oh."

"Well, kind of."

"Oh." He presses down the lever you push to start the heating coils when the bread goes down. It's not plugged in, though. "How do you kind of find somebody?"

"You find out where they are, and it's not here."

"Not even close?" He studies his reflection in the side of the toaster.

"Not even close."

"Oh." He puts it down and looks at me. "So you're sad."

I toss the journal back onto my bunk and sit down next to him. "I guess. Kind of mad, too. I wasted a lot of time looking for him."

Scoop nods.

"What's this for?" I pick up the toaster.

"Mrs. Kennedy brought it to breakfast today."

Shopping Cart Lady. I nod. "Yeah?"

"She thought you could fix it."

I turn the toaster over in my hands and hold up the stripped cord. "It's kind of beat. They have one in the kitchen she can use. She should probably throw this one out."

"She likes this one," Scoop says. "Her husband gave it to her for their wedding."

"Probably a zillion years ago." I toss it on the bed.

"No, thirty-one. She said it was thirty-one years ago this week." Scoop picks it up again and puts it in my lap. "I *told* her you would help."

I look down at the toaster. There's no way I can fix that cord, and who knows what else is wrong inside. The coils are probably shot, too. "Well, it turns out I can't."

Scoop looks up at me. "But I told her you can fix anything."

"I used to think so." I toss the toaster, climb into my own bunk, and push the journal aside.

Scoop climbs up after me.

"Can you give me a little space?" I say. "I'm not having the best week."

"I know. That's why I'm keeping you company." He picks up the journal. "If you didn't find your dad—at least not here anyway—whose journal is this?"

I shrug. "Don't know."

There's a knock at the door. I figure it's Mom, so I yell "Come on in!" And in steps Shopping Cart Lady. She must have left her cart in the dining room.

"Hi, Mrs. Kennedy!" Scoop jumps down from the bunk and gives her a hug. "He won't fix it."

"Oh." She picks up the toaster. She looks sad. "I couldn't bear to get rid of it. So many memories. I was hoping . . ."

While Mrs. Kennedy winds up the cord, I picture her without her shopping cart, looking young and happy with a Mr. Kennedy at a kitchen table in a real house. Maybe even with kids. And then I get why she wants to keep the toaster. She was hoping. Sometimes, that's enough to get you through.

It got me through the past few weeks. In another month, Mom's going to have her degree, and we'll be okay. Dad still won't be here. But we'll be okay.

"Mrs. Kennedy?"

She looks up at the top bunk. "Yes?"

"Keep the toaster," I say. "I'll go to the hardware store and try to find what I'd need to fix that cord. I'm not positive I can fix it, but—" I don't even know what I'm saying. The words spill out. "It's—it's an important toaster. So keep it just in case."

She nods and finishes wrapping the cord. "That's what I'm going to do," she says, and heads for the door. "But I'll tell you this. I'm no fool. I'm still going to find another way to toast my bread."

She leaves, and I almost smile.

I flop back on my bunk, and my head clunks the journal. I pick it up and flip through it.

"Know what I think?" Scoop says.

"What?"

"I think you still want to know who wrote that even though it's not your dad."

"Yeah?"

"Yeah." He says it like one of those tough cowboys in an old western movie, and it makes me laugh.

"Okay, then," I say. "Want to come with me on a secret mission?"

His eyes light up. "Sure!"

"Go tell your mom I'm taking you to the park."

We head out into the sun, and Scoop is step-step-running-skipping to keep up with me. If I'm not back when Mom gets off work, she's going to flip.

"Slow down, will ya?" Scoop jumps off the curb, and I grab his hand to lead him across the street.

"Nope. You have to hurry when you're on a secret mission."

"It's cold out here." Scoop zips his sweatshirt. "I shoulda brought a coat."

"Walk faster. You'll warm up," I say. But he's right. It's getting chillier.

We rush past the huge houses and cross the bridge as fluffy snowflakes start to drift down from the clouds.

"Snow!" Scoop almost falls off the curb trying to catch a flake on his tongue. He makes me think of Gee. She loves those big, fat snowflakes.

"Watch out, will ya?" I take his hand and turn toward the water tower.

And I stop.

Because there he is.

Senior Searcher is sitting on a towel underneath the tower. He's leaning back on his elbows, staring up at the falling snow. Holding my letter in his hands.

CHAPTER 38
Senior Searcher

His long legs stick out like puppet legs in front of him. His hair is gray, almost white. So is his mustache.

"Mr. Webster?"

I shuffle through the dry grass, up to his red-and-yellow striped towel. The red is faded almost to pink.

He lifts his head. "You go by Zig, right?"

I nod.

"I know you from your old paper route. You and that red-haired runner girl were the only kids who were ever up when I went for my walks." He hands me the letter. "I'm not the person you meant this for, am I?"

I shake my head. "But you're Senior Searcher. Right?"

He pulls a GPS unit like mine from the pocket of his jacket. "That I am."

"Hey, can I see that?" Scoop says. Mr. Webster hands it to him, and he starts pressing buttons, a huge smile on his face. I always told him not to touch mine, afraid he'd mess up the coordinates I'd entered.

"I've found fifty-three caches and counting," Mr. Webster says. "I took a break for a while this fall, though."

"This summer, too," I say. "Since the end of June."

He nods slowly. "Yep. Used to be three of us old geezers out looking for treasure together—Dominic, George, and me. Dominic's grandson told him about this geocaching business, and we thought it sounded like a better way to get exercise than wandering around with no place to go. And George was a whiz with electronics, so he got us all set up with the GPS units."

I think about my box of electronics from the garage sale. "Your friend's name is George?"

Mr. Webster gives me a sad smile. "It was. George died a while back, and I got busy with my wife being sick and then . . . well . . . it seemed frivolous to keep playing a silly game." He squints into the morning sun and holds up his hand to block it so he can see my face. "How'd you know I stopped in June? You been following me from cache to cache?"

I nod.

"And you thought Senior Searcher was somebody else. Not some old man wandering around Lakeland to get his steps in." He lifts his sleeve to show me the Fitbit on his wrist. "Doctor says ten thousand steps a day on this sucker will keep my heart healthy."

"Can I see that, too?" Scoop says. Mr. Webster takes it off his wrist. Scoop holds it and starts jumping to make the lights change.

"I thought . . . I actually thought you were my dad," I say finally. "I'm Kirby junior, and he's Kirby senior, so . . ."

"Oh. So you thought Senior Searcher . . ."

Senior Searcher.

Senior *Citizen* Searcher.

I was so sure. It never occurred to me it might not be him.

"I thought it was my dad. Yeah." It sounds so dumb now.

I wait for Mr. Webster to laugh at me, but he doesn't. He reaches into his jacket pocket. "Want a butterscotch?"

"No, thanks."

"I'll have one." Scoop stops jumping with the Fitbit long enough to pop the hard candy into his mouth.

Mr. Webster has one, too. He looks up at the water tower. Clouds are blowing past so fast behind it that it looks like some time-lapse thing in a movie.

"Sorry about that," he says.

"About what?"

"About not being your dad."

"Oh. Well . . . yeah. It's not your fault."

"Have a seat." He slides over to one side of the faded towel, and I sit down.

"Here's your step counter thingy," Scoop says, dropping it

in Mr. Webster's lap. "I got it to ten thousand for you, so you're good for today." He turns to me and points at the base of the tower. "I'm going over there to pick some of those purple flowers for my mom."

"Don't climb," I tell him.

"They're asters," Mr. Webster says. "The last flowers to bloom in the fall."

"Cool," Scoop says, and runs off.

Mr. Webster keeps talking. "Asters are the die-hards. The ones who won't give up no matter how cold the nights get. I like a flower like that."

"That's cool," I say. I pull out Mr. Webster's journal. "Here. This is yours, right?"

His face lights up. "Wow! Thought I'd lost that for good. I must have dropped it on one of my hikes. Where'd you find it?"

"By the marble cache along the lakeshore."

"Gotta watch out for trains on that one," he says.

"Yep. We know."

He flips through the pages. "This thing held up pretty well." He stops at the last entry, reads it. Then looks up at me. "What made you think this was your dad's?"

That is the greatest question ever. What did?

"Well, there were some parts in there where he—I mean, where you—talk about missing L. My mom is Laurie, and they're divorced, so I thought . . ." Was that really all there was? I look down at my sneakers. "I don't know what I thought."

He smiles a little. Sad. "That *L* is for Lucille. My wife."

"Are you divorced, too?"

He shakes his head. "My wife is in a home—a skilled nursing facility. She has Alzheimer's disease. Last summer, she started wandering off and almost—" He nearly chokes on the words. "I can't take care of her anymore."

I don't know what to say. "Sorry."

"Not your fault. Any more than it's my fault I'm not your dad." He tries to smile. "I just wish I could have found a nurse to care for her in our house. There's a shortage of home health care providers. The few that were available cost more than we can afford, and insurance . . ." He shakes his head and then waves off what he started to say. "Ahh. You don't know about insurance."

I think back to the waiting room. The rabies shots. I'm lucky I didn't get sick. "No, I get it. That stinks."

Scoop comes running up with a fistful of flowers—asters. They look like they're celebrating spring, even though we've had two nights of frost this week. "Here," he says, handing half the bouquet to Mr. Webster. "You can have these."

"Thank you," he says, and holds them to his nose. "Lucille and I used to picnic here back when the tower was in use. It was a lot cleaner then. But still with the big, open sky." He looks up, and I follow his eyes. One of the clouds looks like a hippo. "Lucille loved to find shapes in the clouds. She loves wildflowers, too, so I appreciate these, young man." He nods at Scoop.

Tires scrunch on gravel at the side of the road. The engine

dies and Mom gets out, still in her apron. I hear her tips jingling in her pocket from here, which means she didn't even stop at the shelter.

She walks right up to the towel. "Kirby Zigonski, I—"

Scoop jumps up in front of her. "Here!" He thrusts the rest of the flowers at her and blurts out, "They're the toughest flower around."

Mom takes the flowers. She looks at me. She looks at the striped towel. At Mr. Webster. Her eyes drop to the GPS unit in his lap, the little green journal in his hands.

Then she looks back at me. "I told you to stay home this morning."

"Yeah, I know." I don't say it in a snotty way. "I had to come."

Mom surprises me and flops down on the grass.

Mr. Webster starts to stand up. "You can sit on the towel . . ."

But Mom waves away his offer. She holds out her hand. "I'm Laurie Zigonski," she says, and Mr. Webster leans over to shake it.

"It's a pleasure to meet you and your boys," he says. Mom doesn't bother to correct him, and that makes Scoop smile. "I'm Robert Webster." He holds up the GPS unit and shrugs. "Senior Searcher to my friends."

Mom stares at him. Then she stares at me. Then she leans back and looks up at the water tower, and tears stream down her cheeks. She doesn't bother wiping them away.

The whole thing is so weird. So we all just sit there.

"Butterscotch?" Mr. Webster holds one out.

Mom takes it. "Thank you."

"Can I have another one?" Scoop asks. Mr. Webster hands one to him. Scoop curls up in Mom's lap and leans back, too, to watch the clouds.

Now there's one that looks like the state of Oklahoma.

"You want one, too?" Mr. Webster pulls another candy from his pocket. He's like one of those magicians pulling scarves out of a sleeve. How many candies could he possibly have in there?

I take it and look up, right as Oklahoma changes into an alligator in a top hat. I say so. And that makes Scoop laugh. And the candy tastes good.

And somehow, that helps.

Surprises always come in bunches, Mom says.

When we get back to the shelter, Aunt Becka's there with a fresh bruise on her cheek and a box of our stuff in her arms. My garage sale toaster is balanced on top.

Aunt Becka sets it down in room five, takes Mom's hand, and walks with her to the library. They talk in quiet voices. A lot quieter than last time.

I flop down on the lower bunk, pick up the toaster, and loosen the screws that hold the bottom on. It doesn't take much; I didn't tighten them very well last time.

I stare at the connections for less than a minute before I see the problem. It needs to be rewired.

Totally rewired.

With a different kind of circuit. A parallel circuit. And then it should work for years.

How could I have missed it before?

I dig through the box from Aunt Becka's house for spare wire, and I get to work.

The great thing about a parallel circuit is how things work out, even when something goes wrong. You can have ten or even twenty LCD bulbs all strung together, along with an alarm that goes off if a pressure pad gets tripped and makes a connection, and no matter what happens, the electrons manage to make it through. You could have five bulbs burn out and because of the way it's all wired up, there's still a path for the electrons to travel. They find their way. If there's a roadblock, they find another way.

And things work out.

CHAPTER 39

Giving Thanks

"We need more of the fruity cans! You there—" A bony finger taps my shoulder.

"It's me, Nonna. Zig." I put down a gravy ladle and turn so she can see my face.

She frowns at me for a minute. "What kind of name is Zig?"

I try not to sigh. It used to be our big joke that she's the only person who refused to call me by my nickname. She said it made me sound like a cartoon character and that was no name for such a handsome young man. "It's a nickname. Short for Kirby Zigonski. I like to be called Zig. What was it you needed?"

She looks down at her hands and makes them into the shape they'd be if she were holding a can of food. "Fruity cans. We're out of the fruity cans."

"Cranberry sauce, Nonna?" Gianna swoops in with a new

pan of gravy and waits for me to lift the old one. "I'll get more. It's going fast, huh?"

We've already served a couple dozen people, and there are at least that many more in line. It feels busier than usual at the shelter.

Maybe because it's getting colder out every day.

Maybe because it's Thanksgiving and people came for the turkey.

Or maybe because I'm not used to this mishmash of people at meals anymore, even though Mom and I just moved out nine days ago.

"Hey, Zig!" Scoop comes racing over in his new snow boots. There's only a few inches on the ground, but he's excited. "Zig, I've got my speech ready. Wanna hear?"

"It's not really a speech, you know."

"It kind of is," he says. "Wanna hear? I've been practicing."

I told him he should prepare one thing to share at Thanksgiving Grace, when everyone goes around the table to say why they're thankful. Instead, he's written a Nobel Prize acceptance speech.

I stir the gravy. "Go ahead."

"I'd like to thank you all for coming today."

I can't help it. I laugh.

"What?" He looks offended.

"Sorry," I say. "You make it sound like they had so many other invitations to choose from."

I look out over the crowd. Mrs. Kennedy is carefully wrapping up dinner rolls in her napkin and stashing them under her coat on top of the cart. Kevin Richards walks past her and drops more rolls on her plate. She high-fives him. Partners in crime.

Heather has her arm around someone I haven't met—a woman who looks like she might be from India or Pakistan. She's sitting sideways, trying to eat her turkey around her nursing baby. Heather is talking to her. Rob Thomas is talking to a young guy with a guitar. Brother Vinnie is talking to his squash.

"So . . . thank you all for coming today." Scoop looks at me out of the corner of his eye, waiting to see if I laugh again. I don't.

"Thanksgiving can be a happy time and a sad time, too, if you think about stuff you don't have. Like a house. Or an apartment. Or a dad." He glances at me again. I keep stirring gravy. "Sometimes, the things you don't have are all you can think about."

"Know what I don't have, young man?" Brother Vinnie shouts.

"What's that?"

"Gravy! Will ya move it?"

Scoop scoots over to me. I ladle gravy onto Brother Vinnie's mashed potatoes, and he moves on.

"But I'm thankful for what I do have," Scoop says.

"You realize everyone's going to be finished with their pie before you're done?"

"Shh . . . I'm almost finished." He looks down at his paper. I see Heather's neat handwriting. He must have had her write it all down. "I'm thankful for this food. I'm thankful for my bed, even though it's not a top bunk, and for *Library Lion*, and that we're going to be moving soon." He gets a big grin on his face and says, "Next week!"

"I know." I smile right back at him. I felt awful leaving him, so I was glad when Heather told Mom they found an apartment she could afford. She got a job with Stop Domestic Violence, working with other women who need help. Heather has her own business cards and everything. Mom took one for Aunt Becka. She'll probably toss it aside, but you never know.

Scoop rattles his paper dramatically. His big finish. "And I'm thankful for my friends here. Because friends help."

He puts the paper down.

"That's it?"

He nods. "Yeah."

"It's good. Do you want a big ending that ties everything together?"

"I have that," he says. He looks at his paper again. "Friends help." He looks up at me. "Don't you think that's big?"

"Actually, yeah." I guess I do.

"I'll second that!" Mr. Webster steps up with a case of cranberry sauce. "Where does this go?"

"Over there." I point to Nonna. "With the other fruity cans."

Mr. Webster gets it. His wife is down at the end of the buffet table serving dinner rolls with what we call tongs and she calls grabby claws. She reminds me a lot of Gianna's grandmother when she can't remember the names of ordinary things. Mrs. Webster calls our doorbell the "visitor alarm."

When Mom and I first moved in with the Websters, it was hard to get used to. No matter how many times Mr. Webster told his wife that Mom was a registered nurse and was going to be her caregiver, she'd forget. No matter how many times he told her we'd be staying in the two bedrooms down the hall and helping out, she didn't remember. She'd see Mom coming into the kitchen and holler, "Who are you? I didn't hear the visitor alarm! Robert! Somebody's in the house!"

"Need a break from the gravy train?" Mr. Webster takes the ladle. I fill my plate and find Mom at one of the tables.

She pulls out a chair for me. "Hey, kiddo. Glad you're off duty for a while. Volunteers have to eat, too."

I switch on and off between eating and handing Scoop napkins to wipe gravy off his chin. I'm finishing my stuffing when Rob brings out the pies and clinks a spoon against a coffee mug to get everyone's attention.

"Let's have a moment of shared thankfulness." He nods to Scoop, who must have asked about going first. Good for him.

Scoop delivers his speech like he practiced. He makes a dramatic pause right before his big finale. "And I'm thankful for my friends here. Because friends help."

He sits down. Nobody laughs. Mrs. Kennedy starts clapping, and soon everyone else does, too. Brother Vinnie stands up on his chair and goes on clapping a good thirty seconds after the rest of us have stopped.

Then Mr. Webster stands. "I'm thankful for this." He pulls his yellow GPS unit from his jacket pocket. "Because it led a boy to find me sitting under a water tower. I wasn't who he hoped I'd be. But I'm pretty sure I'm who he was supposed to find. Because things have worked out awfully well." He puts his hand on his wife's shoulder, and she looks up at him and smiles. For right now, at least, she knows whose hand it is.

Other people talk about new jobs and new babies and hopes for a different kind of life. I half listen, but I mostly eat pumpkin pie with whipped cream. I'm scraping the plate when a green journal slides onto the table next to it.

"I think you ought to have this," Mr. Webster says.

I shake my head and wipe my mouth. "This has all your geocaches in it and everything. You should keep it."

"This isn't my journal." Mr. Webster flips through the pages. They're blank. "This one's yours. It's time you logged some finds of your own instead of following Senior Searcher all over the place."

I run my hand over the cover. A geocaching journal.

I think about Mr. Webster's entries. Plenty were about hidden Tupperware, but there was more than that. The notes about missing his wife. About dealing with all the changes in his life. Noticing what was around him.

And remembering.

"Thanks," I say. I'll probably write about some of that stuff, too. And make diagrams for my electrical projects.

Mom stands up and gathers her dishes. "We'll have to leave cleanup to the rest of the crew," she says. "I have a shift at the diner before we do dinner at home later."

She leaves, and I turn to Scoop. "You excited about your big move?"

"Really excited. I can't wait to get out of here," he says. "I mean, it was okay when you were here, but . . ."

"Want to read before I go?"

His whole face lights up and he's back at the table with *Library Lion* in about five seconds. "Start at the good part," he says.

"You don't want to hear the whole thing?"

He shakes his head. "I know all the sad parts. Read the good part."

So I do. I make Mr. McBee's voice all deep and official when he invites the lion back to the library. Then I turn the page, and the picture shows the lion coming home.

I look up at Scoop. His smile is even bigger than the lion's.

CHAPTER 40
Skips and Wishes

I take the long way home. I was going to stop at the diner to say hi to Mom. But when I walk by the park, it pulls me in.

I scuff the pebbles. They make cold, crunchy November sounds under the dusting of snow that fell this week. Pretty soon the stones will be iced together, and the lake will be frozen, too. No more rock skipping till spring.

I look up from the rocks as a great blue heron takes off from the point of beach next to the swing set. It flies into the wind, its legs stretched out long behind it.

I sit down on the bench at the edge of the water and fumble in my backpack for a pen. I take out my geocaching journal.

I'm not geocaching today, so this isn't official or anything. But it's something I need to write.

I thought it was you. I thought you were leaving clues for me. All over the place. It seemed like something you would do.

But it wasn't. I guess you know that.

You could have called, you know. Or written. It would have been better than just finding out. And I did, you know. I found out. I know.

You probably realize that, too. But maybe you don't know that I'd still like to talk to you. So write, okay? Or call or something if they let you. I want to talk to you. That was all I ever really wanted. It would have been enough.

I can still see the heron, a tiny flutter against the clouds. Will the guy who wanted to wipe out all those bird nests to make room for condos understand any of this? Maybe not. But I sign it anyway.

Circuit Boy

No.

Zig Junior

No.

Just *Zig*.

I'll send it tonight, now that Mom's given me the address for the prison.

Maybe he'll answer. Maybe not.

That's okay. Sometimes maybe has to be enough because it's all you get.

I rip out the page, fold it, and tuck it into the front pocket of my backpack.

"Hey! You're here!" Ruby calls, bounding off the curb. Gianna's right behind her. "We wondered where you went."

"Mom had to work, so I'm swinging by the diner before I go back to the Websters' place."

"Back *home*," Gianna corrects me.

I smile. Mr. Webster keeps saying that, too. I guess it is home. It's starting to feel like it. Looking back, I feel so dumb about not telling Gianna and Ruby what was going on. But when everything you've ever known falls out from under you, the whole world seems less friendly. We talked about it over pizza one night. I said I was sorry, and Gee said she understood, and she was sorry, too. She and Ruby had been keeping their own secret—about my dad. They knew where he was before I did, but they didn't feel like I should find out from them. I don't know. I might have done the same thing if I were them. Nobody wants to share that kind of news.

"You know what?" Ruby bends down and picks through the pebbles. "It's a good day for skipping." She wanders down the beach, leaving me alone with Gianna.

Gee picks up a nice, flat rock. "Ready?"

I look out at the waves. They're all choppy, and dotted with gobs of snow and slush. It is so not a good day for skipping.

But I have a wish in mind. There's another school dance next month. Another chance. So I start looking for a stone.

"Wait! Use this one." Gianna tugs on my backpack. I bend

down so she can unzip the front pocket, the small one where she tucked my perfect skipping rock. It's still there.

"Here." She drops it in my hand, and I feel its smooth weight in my palm. I run my thumb over the stone and wrap my finger around the edge. I curl my arm in. Tuck my wrist into my chest. And let go.

The rock bounces off the first wave. It takes a right turn and hits another wave square on. Then it skips and skips and skips.

Read on for a sneak peek at Kate Messner's new novel, a
fast-paced, thought-provoking story told through letters,
poems, text messages, news stories, and comics.

Saturday, June 8—
Letter from Nora Tucker
(Whatever you do, don't
skip this one, because
we actually have something
to report now!!)

Dear future Wolf Creek residents,

BREAKING NEWS: **TWO INMATES BROKE OUT OF DAD'S PRISON OVERNIGHT!!!**

Seriously! Lizzie and I were working on our newspaper articles last night, and we went to bed at around ten. Then at eight this morning, the doorbell rang, and it was a state trooper who told Mom about the breakout. Mom already knew, though, because I guess Dad got a phone call at five this morning, when they were discovered missing, so he had to go to work then.

(By the way, you know those alarms on the prison towers that are supposed to go off to warn everybody if inmates break out? Yeah, they totally didn't go off. I don't know if they'll be fixed by the time you're reading this or not, but I wouldn't count on them if I were you.)

Anyway, Mom told Lizzie and me not to say anything to Owen because she doesn't want him to be scared. Mom says this isn't going to last very long because it's June in the mountains, so even if the police don't find those guys right away, it won't be long before the blackflies do, and then they'll be begging to go back to their cells. (Do you still get blackflies in the woods every June? Maybe by the time you read this, you'll have found a way to get rid of them, and if that's the case, you're lucky because they're mean little things. Dad says they're vampires with wings.)

Mom also told us she got an early-morning call from Lizzie's mom, who's at the hospital with Lizzie's grandma. Her grandma was supposed to go to work this morning—she's a civilian worker at the prison—but I guess she woke up with chest pains, so they went to the emergency room to have her checked out. She's fine—it wasn't a heart attack or anything—but they're still at the hospital, so Lizzie's mom can't pick her up until later.

And that reminds me—I got that recipe for you from Lizzie's grandma:

Priscilla's Magical Minty Brownies

1. Mix up two packages of any brand fudge brownie mix according to the directions.

2. Pour a little less than half the mix into a 10 x 15 inch baking dish.

3. Put a layer of York Peppermint Patties on top of that.

4. Pour the rest of the mix over it and bake at 350 degrees for about 45 minutes or until they seem done.

I was expecting something fancier, but I guess that was the secret of her secret recipe. Sometimes things aren't quite how they seem.

Anyway, back to the prison break. Lizzie and I wanted to go out reporting, but Mom said no because of the manhunt happening now. I told her I think that's pretty unfair, since Sean was allowed to go to the market for work, but she didn't care. I kind of wish college was still in session so Mom would have less time to worry and make new rules. Unfortunately, she gets to work from home a lot of the time until it gets busy again in August.

So now Lizzie and I are going to collect background information instead. Our school paper adviser says that's important to have in news stories so readers can see how what's happening now fits into the bigger picture. So Lizzie's making some charts about the prison, showing the population and stuff, and I'm collecting all my notes about Alcatraz history from my book research so we can compare the two escapes. There are some pretty cool stories from Alcatraz. One team of guys who tried to escape made dummies and left them in their beds so it would look like they were sleeping instead of running around free. Pretty smart, right? More to come . . .

Your friend from the past,

Nora Tucker

Saturday, June 8—
Text messages between
Lizzie & her mom,
8:45 a.m.

MOM: You up yet?

LIZZIE: Yes how's grandma?

MOM: Ok docs say it's not heart related. Just anxiety

LIZZIE: That's good

MOM: They want to run more tests so are you ok staying with Nora again if they keep her overnight tonight?

LIZZIE: Sure

Hey did you hear about the prison break?

MOM: Yes but doctor is here so I have to go. I'll keep you posted Love you!

LIZZIE: Love u too

Saturday, June 8—
Recorded conversation,
9:00 a.m.

NORA: What are you doing? I thought you were gonna work on
charts and stuff.

LIZZIE: I will. I'm recording a conversation first.

NORA: ~~Yahoo~~ You ought to save the batteries, so we can use it when we go
out later.

LIZZIE: Your mom's ~~now leading a sow~~ not letting us out until those guys are
caught.

NORA: She might ~~lead her~~ later if we're with Sean. Come on. Save
space so we can record stuff at the market.

LIZZIE: I will. I just want to test that app Sean told us about.

NORA: ~~Doesn't~~ Does it listen and turn the audio file into words?

LIZZIE: That's the idea. But the reviews ~~also~~ ^{all say} you might need to correct stuff later.

NORA: Okay. But do you have enough now? Because you should work on the charts, and I'm gonna stop talking so I can find my Alcatraz stuff.

LIZZIE: Yeah, this should be good. This is Lizzie and Nora, ~~over a noun.~~ over and out!

LIZZIE'S REFLECTIONS: The app worked! Mostly, anyway. I had to type in who's saying what, because obviously the app doesn't know us. Also, after I printed this out, I noticed that it made some mistakes. It had Nora's mom "leading a sow" (Ha!) but I corrected those in pen. Sorry about that. I'll fix them on the computer before I print next time. The app reviews all say that it works better once it gets used to your voice, so hopefully there won't be much to correct anyway. My reflection is that I'm really glad this works now and I hope our next recorded conversation is more exciting. I have to go now because Nora says we have to use this time to get all the "background information" for the story.

Saturday, June 8—
Lizzie's chart and
timelines about prison
history and population
and stuff, for
background

WOLF CREEK CORRECTIONAL FACILITY TIMELINE

(These notes are from the Department of Corrections website, Nora's History Day report from last year, and Wikipedia, which I know is not a 100 percent reliable source, but we're not allowed to go to the library because we're locked in the house, so that's as good as it gets tonight.)

1850	Opens as a mining prison—inmates work in mines nearby
1892	Prison expands to hold maximum security inmates
1899	5 inmates try to escape—it doesn't work out for them
1908	Construction begins on concrete wall all around prison property
1910	Construction complete (it's a REALLY big wall)
1910-this week	Wall keeps inmates inside prison
June 7	BREAKOUT! 2 inmates escape overnight, discovered missing at 5 a.m. the next day
June 8	Police still looking for guys who broke out TO BE CONTINUED

WOLF CREEK CORRECTIONAL STATISTICS
(Source: NY Department of Corrections & Census Bureau)

Population of Wolf Creek, NY: 3,261

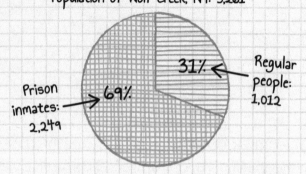

31% ← Regular people: 1,012

Prison inmates: 2,249 → 69%

Wolf Creek Correctional Inmate Demographics
(this means people's backgrounds & stuff)

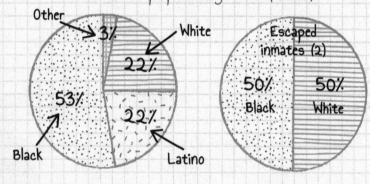

Other → 3%

White ← 22%

53% Black

22% ← Latino

Escaped inmates (2)

50% Black

50% White

Wolf Creek Correctional Facility Officers

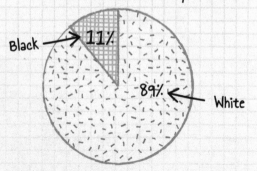

Black → 11%

89% ← White

LIZZIE'S REFLECTIONS: I've always known Wolf Creek is a small town with a big prison, but I've never realized that most of our town is made up of inmates. There are more than twice as many people living in that prison as there are out here. That's weird. But it goes to show how cool pie charts are. They help you see things.

Another thing these charts made me see is that more than half the prison population is black but almost none of the corrections officers are. I'm wondering if that's right or if it's a typo on the website, so I'm going to ask Grandma about this when she gets out of the hospital. Hopefully, that'll be first thing tomorrow. Mom says whatever it was, she's much better and just getting some rest now before she comes home.

Most famous Alcatraz escape attempt—Frank Morris,
John Anglin & Clarence Anglin in 1962

- ★ Sharpened tools & used them to dig out of their cells
- ★ Went down to water
- ★ Made inflatable raft out of raincoats (???HOW???)
- ★ Launched homemade raft into bay
- ★ Probably drowned (but nobody knows for sure . . .)

Other guys who tried to escape from Alcatraz:

Joe Bowers   1936
Theodore Cole & Ralph Roe   1937
Thomas Limerick   1938

TO BE CONTINUED LATER BECAUSE MOM JUST
CAME IN & SAID WE CAN GO TO THE MARKET AS
LONG AS WE'RE HOME BY DINNERTIME!

KATE MESSNER is a former middle-school English teacher and the author of the E. B. White Read Aloud Award winner *The Brilliant Fall of Gianna Z.*, *Sugar and Ice*, *Eye of the Storm*, *Wake Up Missing*, *All the Answers*, *The Seventh Wish*, *The Exact Location of Home*, *Breakout*, *Capture the Flag*, *Hide and Seek*, the Marty McGuire and Ranger in Time chapter book series, and several picture books. She lives on Lake Champlain with her husband and two kids. When she's not reading or writing, she loves hiking, kayaking, biking, and watching thunderstorms over the lake.

www.katemessner.com
@KateMessner

From **high-stakes** adventure
to **unexpected** magic
to **sweet** friendships—
there's a lot to love
from Kate Messner!